ABOUT THIS BOOK

Welcome to the secluded mountain town of Havenwood Falls, home to sexy men, strong women, and neighbors who bite. Discover supernatural mystery, thrills, and romance in a place where everyone has a deep, dark, and often deadly secret.

Nineteen-year-old Ember Ramsey creates trouble everywhere she goes, and right now, she's on the warpath. Driven to avenge her momma's brutal murder, she infiltrates a world of bloodthirsty monsters, but as a flame-wielding fighter, she might be the deadliest of them all. When she enters a fight club in Denver to squeeze information out of a known snitch, she comes face to face with the black-eyed demon who haunts her nightmares.

With her mark finally in sight, Ember trails the killer to a quaint mountain town. But when her welcoming committee includes a nosy rent-a-cop, a cocky local with suspicious connections, and a whole slew of supernaturals living side by side, Ember realizes that Havenwood Falls is no ordinary town. Finding her momma's killer just got a whole lot harder.

Never before has Ember been so close to her goal, but with each step she takes, her control weakens. Soon the fires will spread, and Ember is no longer sure she can hold back the incredible power she possesses. Or that she wants to—even if it means burning Havenwood Falls to the ground.

FROM THE EMBERS

A HAVENWOOD FALLS NOVELLA

AMY MILES

HAVENWOOD FALLS BOOKS

Forget You Not by Kristie Cook

Old Wounds by Susan Burdorf

Fate, Love & Loyalty by E.J. Fechenda

Covetousness by Randi Cooley Wilson

The Winged & the Wicked by T.V. Hahn & Kristie Cook

Alpha's Queen by Lila Felix

Ink & Fire by R.K. Ryals

Lose You Not by Kristie Cook

Tragic Ink by Heather Hildenbrand

Nowhere to Hide by Belinda Boring

Flames Among the Frost by Amy Hale

Rock Me Gently by Susan Burdorf

From the Embers by Amy Miles

Defying Gravity by Kallie Ross

Gypsy Heart by Randi Cooley Wilson

Break Me Not by Kristie Cook

More books releasing on a monthly basis

Also try the YA line, Havenwood Falls High

Stay up to date at www.HavenwoodFalls.com

To all of the dreamers out there still waiting for their moment to shine.

Now is your moment. Shine on!

CHAPTER 1

*S*mart people knew to duck when the world took a swing at them. I guess I hadn't learned that lesson yet. Taking a hit was something I knew how to do. Knowing when to stop before my luck ran out—well, that was another story.

A cheer rose from the crowd. My hair blocked the view of the approaching wall, but I sure felt it. With a groan, I collapsed into the gutter. The murky water tasted of rotting trash, and I didn't want to think of what else. I spit to the side before I rolled to my back.

That one hurt.

"You sure you're up for another round, Ember?" Two glowing orb-like eyes stared down at me. They looked far too small compared to the eggplant-sized nose they flanked. "You're lookin' a bit rough after Fluffy took that last chunk out of you."

The troll wasn't wrong.

A single tear rolled down my cheek, and I caught it with my fingertip. It shimmered there like a summer sunset against the night. The instant I touched it to the gouge in my right side, sweet relief rushed in. Having healing powers sure came in handy.

"Whoever named that seven-foot-tall bastard of a skinwalker Fluffy deserves to have their head kicked in," I said.

I'd been fighting against scum like him for six years, but he was my first skinwalker. The stories were few and far between. Some relayed tales

AMY MILES

of creatures that could assume the skin of a man instead of a beast. Staring up at Fluffy's three heads, I wished I'd taken on one of them instead.

Fuzzbert laughed. "That's my girl."

The hand that yanked me to my feet was the size of a large serving platter, dotted with tufts of hair. It was a tight squeeze to escape around his belly. The friction of his wet poncho trapped me. I wiggled free and leaned against the wall to catch my breath.

There were dozens of wounds in need of healing, but they would have to wait. Fluffy paced, watching me. Saliva dripped in thick strings from his gaping jaws. Blood matted the soaked fur near one of his right eyes and his hind leg. It was hard to tell which of his three heads was the dominant one. They were all glaring at me with blackened hatred through the rain.

Fluffy made the hound of Hades look like a puppy. Not exactly fair in hand-to-hand combat, but most street-fighting clubs didn't have rules. At least not rules that went in favor of anyone but the man in charge. Or rather the troll in charge, in this case.

Like most in the crowd, Fuzzbert waited for me to call the fight. Like heck was I tapping out. A lot of money was riding on this.

But I wasn't here for the money.

"Ember?" Fuzzbert stepped toward me. He cast a wary glance at the sky. Trolls didn't like lightning.

I held up my hand. "I need a minute to breathe."

That last hit was the hardest I'd ever taken. Fluffy must have been on steroids. Or a drug that was less than legal.

I'd fared well enough against two of his heads, but that third one literally bit me in the backside. It was a shame they confiscated my dagger at the start of the fight. I'd love to stake one of his heads to the wall.

"Time's up, Ember." The crowd pressed in closer to hear Fuzzbert. They were a rainbow of colors, each with ponchos of various sizes. Folks in Denver sure took their fight clubs seriously. "Are you tapping out?"

Wiping a mixture of blood and rain from my brow, I grinned and thumped Fuzzbert on his warty nose.

"If you were half as smart as you are ugly, you'd already know the answer to that."

Fuzzbert's breath wheezed around the gap in his lips. Crooked teeth, as long as my fingers, jutted from his gums.

2

"Speak for yourself." His laugh sounded like an old lady who'd smoked for three lifetimes.

"Aw, come on, Fuzz. You know it's not nice to make a girl cry," I said.

I wasn't as ugly as a troll, but I wasn't a beauty queen either, thanks to a run-in I had a few years ago with fire. Turns out healing tears did squat on that.

Fluffy's hackles rose at the first rumble of thunder in the distance. He squared off with me. A sharp bark sent the crowd back to clear the area.

"That mutt has got a hair up his backside tonight." Fuzzbert might look menacing to most, but I knew his sweet spot. He loved money. It didn't matter how he got it.

I palmed him the last bit of cash I had to my name. "I need some information. He's going to give it up, one way or another."

The troll shook his head. "It's your funeral."

"You'd better be careful, Fuzz." I tied my hair back into a semblance of a bun. "Someone might think you've gone soft on a human."

He snorted and stomped away. If I wasn't paying so well, he'd probably eat me for that comment.

"Hurry up. Place your bets." Fuzzbert cast a scowl at the clouds. "I haven't got all night."

I leaned against the wall, trying to appear unconcerned as Fluffy paced. There wasn't much room in the back alley for the two of us, let alone the crowd that had gathered. Fluffy had a fat butt, which slowed him down. His love of cupcakes and the forty years he had on me didn't help him much. The thinner air up here in Denver wasn't exactly treating me well, either.

"I'm going to gnaw your bones into splinters." Fluffy's words came out in a raspy snarl.

If it weren't for Fuzz warning me ahead of time that Fluffy was a skinwalker, I'd have been shocked the first time he spoke.

"I always wondered if your kind eats humans." I pretended to shudder. "That's cannibalism, you know?"

He clawed the ground.

"Tell me who you work for, Fluffy, and I may let you walk away from this fight."

His growl vibrated in my chest. "I work for no man."

"Man? Nah, I'm looking for a demon with black soulless eyes, a fancy suit, and a thing for stealing young girls."

3

The golden glow of his eyes dimmed. "That describes quite a few of my friends."

"Yes, but you're the lapdog for only one of them," I said.

The upper lip of his middle head curled back to reveal a set of wicked canines. I had no intention of tangling with those again.

"Suit yourself." I pushed off the wall to saunter toward him.

He watched the sway of my hips in the tight leather pants I wore. The metal clasps of my biker boots jingled with each step. The shredded remains of my black tank hung from my chest. A new layer of skin had begun to form over his telltale claw marks.

Fluffy sniffed the air when I stopped less than five feet from him. His sneeze coated me with slime.

"Gross." I wiped my face clean.

"I knew it. I suspected earlier that you weren't human." All three heads dipped low to glare at me. "I'm allergic to only one creature: birds."

I met his condemning gaze. "Do I look like a bird to you?"

"You're a shifter."

I laughed. "If I were, don't you think I would've shifted by now?"

He rolled his eyes to look back at Fuzzbert. "You may not be a shifter, but you aren't human, either."

I'd always known I was different. Healing wasn't the only ability I possessed. I also had a way with fire.

"What's it to you?" I crossed my arms and jutted out one hip.

His laugh made the hair on the back of my neck rise. "Foolish girl. A skinwalker's bite leaves more than a scar."

"You son of a—" My arms fell to my sides. "You bit me, knowing I'd turn into your kind?"

It was sickening, barbaric even. It was also annoyingly brilliant. Not that I would tell him that.

"You chose me as your opponent, remember?" His heads fell in line with each other so his statement sounded in stereo. "The risk was yours to take."

"Bastard," I muttered under my breath. I took hold of his center head. His fur crawled with bugs where I buried my hands to reach the skin. "Give me a name."

Heat flooded into my palms. It started with a familiar tingle but rapidly built to a blistering heat. Steam rose from his wet pelt. The wolf's laugh cut off, and his screams began.

The teeth of his left head sank deep into my arm. Blood flowed around the wounds. His hindquarters slammed into the alley wall. Mortar gave way in chunks, coating his back.

"What's going on over there?"

Fuzzbert's heavy footsteps headed our way.

"Give me his name." I tightened my grip, and the scent of burning fur filled my nose. Pain flared in my shoulder when Fluffy's third head attacked. His teeth ripped at muscle and scored bone. The pain made my vision darken, but I held on.

"Let him go," Fuzzbert demanded.

"Stay out of this, Fuzz. I don't want to hurt you."

"Hurt me?" The troll rocked to a stop. "Have you lost your ever-loving mind, girl? I could grind you into dust in seconds."

I released one hand holding Fluffy and pointed it at Fuzz. Fire erupted in the palm of my hand. A swirling ball of vibrant orange hovered there. In the very center of the flames was a blue so bright, it forced Fuzzbert to look away.

"What are you?" the troll asked from behind the shield of his hand.

That I didn't know. I'd spent years looking for the answer. So far, all I had were questions.

"Get her off me," Fluffy whimpered.

Where I'd gripped Fluffy, the imprint of my palm was beginning to heal. I needed to remain in constant contact with him.

Fuzzbert inched forward. With each step he took, the flames rose higher from my hand. "I don't want any trouble, Fuzz."

"You've got a fine way of showing that."

I broke eye contact with Fluffy to look at the troll. "This man knows who killed my momma. I'm not leaving until he gives me a name."

"Bugger." Fuzzbert rubbed the back of his head, forgetting that he wore a poncho.

"Don't just stand there. Do something!" Fluffy moaned.

Digging my nails into Fluffy's neck drew out a terrible howl. The heat cauterized on contact. His eyes rolled back. The scent of his burnt hair was thick in the air.

Murmurs rippled through the crowd. Several pressed against the protective barrier hiding us from the humans. The mages on Fuzzbert's payroll had to work harder to keep us hidden.

No amount of warding could shield Fluffy's frenzy. His thrashing sent tremors through the concrete. Screeching yelps of pain echoed out of the alley. The doorman standing in front of the small condo building across the street peered into the dark. He couldn't see us. Not yet, at least.

"This is getting out of hand," the troll said, surveying his paying crowd. He was losing them. "Tell her what she wants to know, then bite her head off."

The wolf's eyes glistened with tears. "He'll kill me for saying!"

Fuzzbert gave him a withering glare. "If you finish her off, no one will know but you and me. My silence comes at a very fair price."

That was loyalty for you. It started and ended with the highest bidder.

The stench of fear and urine rose from Fluffy. I wondered if the enchantment could hide that smell, too.

"You'll let me live?" He yipped as flames curled the ends of his fur, spreading out from my hands.

I'd heard my fair share of the tales of his exploits in the human world. He was filth, undeserving of life. But he still had his uses.

I nodded, not trusting myself to say the words in case I changed my mind later. Fluffy sniffed and raised one head, turning it in the direction of the crowd.

"They won't help you," I said and followed his gaze. The vampires in attendance might pay a good price for Fluffy's blood if I decided to fry him.

I wonder if he would taste like a human or an animal to them.

I knew very little about the Navajo legends of such creatures. Only that they were once human—witches who turned only after killing someone close to them. Or at least, that was one rumor floating around. This particular legend was very sensitive to the Native American tribes. So, during my travels, I steered far away from it, out of respect.

There were a couple of shifters in the group that might attack if I did kill him. Even though a skinwalker wasn't the same species, they might stick together. I'd seen pack mentality cross species lines before.

"Quiet!" Fuzzbert shouted to the nervous crowd. Whatever he was trying to hear, I was sure his elephant ears would pick it up. "I hear it, too."

It took another minute for me to hear the sirens.

"Who called the pigs?" A tiny faerie of some sort, sitting on the shoulder of a man at the front, fluttered her wings with agitation.

"Maybe they aren't coming our way." A small goblin beside the faerie

6

wrung his hands. He wore a little suit coat. The glint of a golden pocket watch caught my eye. Fuzzbert was too panicked to notice this tempting treasure.

Another flare from my hand sent Fluffy into spasms hard enough to crack the brick wall. The metal scaffolding fixed to the front of the building collapsed to the street. A great puff of dust burst across the entrance to the alleyway. Pieces of the historic landmark crumbled. The doorman dove for the phone, ensuring that the police would be coming.

That was exactly the advantage I needed.

CHAPTER 2

"This is not a drill. Get to your assigned escape routes." Fuzzbert fisted handfuls of cash into the front of his pants. Several bills floated in the puddle at his feet. "And no refunds!"

Chaos erupted. The instant Fluffy's extra head released its grip on my shoulder, I knew he was going to make a run for it.

"Not so fast, furball." I tossed a flame at his third head to redirect his momentum. "I still need that name."

"You're insane. Those cops will be on us in minutes," he said. "We gotta get out of here."

Wings, paws, and claws beat against the bottleneck at the end of the alley. Fuzzbert should have known better than to pick a location with only one exit—a fact he was now grumbling about as he launched a panther shifter out of his way. He bowled through the crowd and charged across the street. Even with his glamour enchantment in place, he was one butt-ugly woman.

"You're not scared, are you?" I wedged myself around Fluffy so I could grab his tail, but it swung out of reach.

He didn't have to answer me. The scent of his fear was rancid in my nose, burning my eyes.

"I can't be here." His black fur trembled as I gripped his neck. If he shook me free now, he'd have a chance to regain his strength.

"What's the big deal? Can't you just shift?" I'd heard rumors that

Fluffy didn't perform well under pressure. "Is someone having performance anxiety?"

His snarl sent my hair into a whirlwind of tangles. I blew it away to level him with a glare.

"I reckon you might find a way to shift by the time the cops show." I raked scorching nails across his side. He screamed. "Give me a name, or I'll show them my bite marks. They put mutts down for stuff like that."

In hindsight, poking a cornered skinwalker wasn't the smartest idea. But then again, it wasn't exactly out of character, either.

Fluffy turned on me faster than I anticipated. Two sets of teeth pierced flesh, one in my left thigh and the other around my neck. If I'd been human, I'd have bled out. But my body's natural healing powers kicked in.

"Are you kidding me?" I spat blood onto the ground. "That was a cheap shot, even for you."

Searing heat exploded from my palms, setting Fluffy's entire flank alight. His shriek echoed in my ears as he scraped his side—and me right along with it—along the wall. The brick tore at my skin.

Fluffy bounced and twirled as I sent flames flying in unpredictable directions. Disoriented and in pain, he trampled over a nymph. A second one scurried out of his way. The goblin took a hard hit from Fluffy's tail and slammed into the wall. His pocket watch rolled into the street as the creature crumpled and fell still.

A well-aimed flame sent Fluffy's hind leg collapsing to the ground. Planting my boot in the crook of his leg, I hoisted myself onto his back. He bucked like a wild stallion.

"End this," I screamed, tossing another flame at the head of the alley to block his escape.

Fluffy was beyond reasoning with now. Pain and fear made his hackles rise around me. His heads came up, biting and tearing. There was no way to defend myself and hold on at the same time. Squeezing my knees into his sides, I tossed flames at each of his heads.

But that third head did me in again. Razor sharp teeth buried into my thigh. With his mighty tug, I hurtled over the heads of the fleeing creatures and into the street. I landed hard, earning road rash in more places than I cared to count. I rolled several times, then slammed into a Rolls Royce. The driver's side door buckled under the impact.

"Son of a—" I pushed to my feet.

The glamour surrounding the alley faded as the last mage fled. Fluffy was in mid-shift. One of his heads was already gone. The second disappeared into a gaping hole of fur. Bones shattered and then mended as he shrank in size.

"That's disgusting." I held my stomach, sure that if I stuck around to listen to the full transformation, I'd be ill. I'd seen shifters before, but their transitions were more fluid. This was nauseating.

The instant irises began to replace the blacks of his eyes, I knew the cops wouldn't arrive in time to capture him. If that happened, I would lose any advantage I'd fought and bled to gain.

"Oh, no you don't!" I swayed on my feet. Everything hurt now. Blood soaked my clothes. My head felt like I'd had a few too many sips of a spiked witch's brew.

"Fluffy!" My scream made the skinwalker whirl around.

He was not much larger than a Great Dane now. I ran straight at him, flames swirling around my hands. It didn't matter that I was visible. The streets were empty of all but the supernatural. Even the doorman had abandoned his post.

Fluffy raced to the back of the alley. With no way to escape, he turned and bared his teeth.

"You might have stood a chance if you'd stayed full size," I said. My flames lit the space, revealing him pacing in the corner.

"Leave it alone, girl. I'm warning you. You don't know what you're getting yourself mixed up in." His voice had lost much of its gruff tone. With each second that passed, he began to sound more human.

"I don't have a choice." I stalked toward him. "Your boss killed my momma. Tried to steal me. I'm only alive to seek justice."

"Justice?" He snorted. "Men like him don't pay for their crimes. They just go on inflicting new pain."

My hands flexed at my sides, but I didn't attack. "You sound like you can relate."

The wolf's body quivered, and it lowered its head. A moan rippled through the alley. "Not everyone has a choice in who they serve."

That made me stop. "You're a victim too, aren't you?"

Sadness filled the animal's eyes when he looked up at me. "If he wanted you as bad as you say, then run. Get as far from here as you can. He always finds his prey. Always."

I blinked. "So I was right. He is in Denver."

Fluffy's irises lightened to a dingy brown. The whites of his eyes began to return.

"Tell me his name." I rushed forward, desperate to hear those two little words. A name was a small thing. But the price that confession would cost the skinwalker might be higher than I'd imagined.

"I can't." His head swayed back and forth. Another moan escaped his elongated throat but it was not brought on by his shifting. "There's so much more you don't understand—"

"Nakai!"

I turned at the shout. A solitary man stood next to the dented door of the Rolls Royce. The streetlamp highlighted the salt-and-pepper tones of his hair. Deep lines surrounded eyes as black as the night around us. A fine suit clothed his muscular frame.

I knew his face. It had aged, but not enough for me to forget the man who killed my momma.

"Have you been fighting in the streets again like a common mutt?" The man brushed his hand over the dented door. "You'll be paying for this damage in full, I assure you that. Now leave the girl and come along. We have work to do."

"No." This time, Fluffy spoke as a man instead of the beast.

"No?" The killer's eyes narrowed. He swept his gaze in my direction. I instinctively moved toward him.

"Run, girl!"

I glanced back over my shoulder to see the skinwalker in his human form for the first time. He was Nakai now, a Native American man of stunning beauty, apart from the hollowness in his eyes.

He stood without a stitch of clothing on. Burnt flesh spread along his chest and side. Long black hair fell across his shoulders, the ends still smoking. Three full-length pelts lined his back, one head draped on each shoulder and the third over his own head. Now I understood how he was able to transform into a three-headed wolf.

In human form, I doubted he would survive long from his injuries. Death might be preferable now that his boss had discovered him.

My momma's killer stopped short at the skin walker's shout. When his gaze swept between us, recognition lit his eyes. "You!"

Before I could sprint toward the man, he raised his hand. I spied the briefest glow of light before a bullet spiraled toward me. A blinding light exploded out of me before my mind could process that I'd been shot at.

Nakai's scream cut off. A two-story wall of flames scorched everything in its path and burst from the alley.

Glass panes from the second-floor windows melted and dripped from above. The mortar burst apart, forming huge holes in the wall. Pieces of the building stung as they split open my cheek and buried in my arms. Streetlamps became twisted metal lumps, plunging the alley into darkness. Smoke rose from the smoldering heap of the Rolls Royce. The face of the condo building was black with soot.

There was no sign of my momma's killer. In the blink of an eye, he'd vanished.

I never felt the bullet that tore through my arm. Never felt the flames die out as I collapsed.

My head lolled to the side. It took immense effort to breathe as I stared at a pile of dust where Nakai had stood. A set of teeth with two large canines perched on top. The tip of a bullet stuck out from the center of the dust.

But it was not the bullet that killed Fluffy. It was me.

"He wasn't shooting at me," I whispered, reaching for the bullet.

Nakai had known something. Information I wasn't supposed to get my hands on.

The first glow of the police lights flickered against the brick wall as the dust began to settle. The sirens sounded muffled and distorted. A face hovered over mine, and I swam in and out of consciousness.

One thought kept me lucid. I'd seen my momma's killer.

He was long gone by now, lost to me again. But he had been here. This was the closest I'd ever come to finding him. I would hunt him again.

The police swarmed around me where I lay in the epicenter of devastation. The police report would likely say the commotion had been caused by a gas explosion. Tales of strange aftershocks from Fluffy's earlier prancing would be written off as a gas bubble on the move. There would be little that could explain away his cries of pain, but I knew humans well enough. They would convince themselves it was only their imagination.

I would be the only living witness to the events, and I wasn't going to say anything.

Closing my eyes, I tried to focus my healing energies on several places at once. Having the cops interrogate me about bite marks would delay things. It was better to make it look like I'd been in the explosion. Wrong place. Wrong time.

As healing energy ran along my nerve endings, I opened my eyes. I blinked several times, sure that I was hallucinating. Seared into the brick above Fluffy's remains was the blackened shape of a large bird. Exactly where my shadow would have been.

The shape of a firebird.

CHAPTER 3

*M*y head hurt when I woke. Not from my injuries, mind you. I had developed a high pain threshold years ago. What wounds still lingered would heal soon enough. This headache was from the stupid drugs the doctors pumped through my IV They always made me feel hung over.

"You messed yourself up pretty bad this time." The voice was calm and came from the chair seated next to my bed.

"Hey, Susan," I said.

No matter where I found myself in the country, somehow she was always there when I woke up in a hospital. I'd lost count of how many wards I'd visited since she took me in two years back. Or how many airline miles she'd racked up on my account.

Fostering a troubled kid a year before she aged out of the system took a huge heart. Susan Wick had the biggest one I'd ever known. Apart from my momma, of course. Once I turned eighteen, I should've been out on my own. Susan insisted I stick around till I got my footing and all that. She loved me, but also knew admitting that would be awkward for me.

So I used her as a home base of sorts, coming and going as I pleased while I hunted. I didn't have anywhere else to call home. She was the only family I had.

Susan placed her hand on mine, and I closed my eyes. I hated disappointing her.

"I'm sorry," I whispered. And I was.

I wasn't sorry that I'd run away. Or that I'd hitchhiked my way to Denver. Or even that I'd damaged half a city block. I was sorry that I made her worry again.

"Did you find him?" she asked.

I opened my eyes to stare at the ceiling. In the off-white texture, I could picture every detail about him, right down to the dark circles under his eyes. Susan knew I was hunting my momma's killer. Past that, there was only so much truth a human could take.

"I saw him," I said. "He was standing at the end of the alley."

She sighed and leaned back. The plastic chair creaked under her weight. "I suppose I'm not surprised. You're the most stubborn little lady I know."

Stubborn was putting it nicely. Though we never spoke about it, she knew there was something off about me. She'd seen plenty of scrapes and bruises heal overnight while I lived with her. A lesser woman might've worried about an impromptu visit from social services, but not Susan. She had faith.

Not just in God. But in me.

I wished that I could tell her that I wasn't involved in that alley mess. That it had been an unfortunate accident, but I couldn't lie to her. So I said nothing at all.

"What are you going to do now?" she said.

Tension lingered in my healing muscles as I blew out a long breath. I'd need another day before the pain faded. A day more to return to my normal self.

"I can't give up now, Sue." I needed her to understand that.

"I know, darlin'." She squeezed my fingers, ignoring the bindings that held my wrists to the bedrail. One look at my extensive police record would explain the straps. Lifting my head, I spotted the officer standing by my door with his hand on his holster.

"Looks like I have company again." I laughed.

Susan smiled. "You seem to collect admirers wherever you go."

It was a sad smile. One that filled me with guilt so acidic, I wondered if it would burn right through my chest. I deserved that, for what I'd put her through.

"You gonna stop me?" I rolled my head to look at my foster mom for the first time.

There were patches of gray at her temples that hadn't been there before

I arrived at her home. Her pale skin looked paper thin in the dim glow of the light behind my bed. She seemed far older than her fifty-seven years. Jetlag didn't do that. Being in my life did.

"Let's call it an early birthday gift." She laced her fingers through mine. "You're a fine young woman, Ember. I'd love nothing more than for you to come home with me, but I know you too well. This is where you need to be."

My heart swelled with love. Susan didn't need to know the gory details of my past to understand how important this was. Every terrible situation I'd found myself in was because of that black-eyed bastard. I'd done plenty of things I wasn't proud of to find him, but apart from hurting her, I could justify them.

I'd spent my teen years convincing myself that there was some purpose to all of this. I needed to believe my momma didn't die for nothing. The older I got, the more I realized there was a reason. It just wasn't one I was sure I could live with.

That man came for me.

I was different. A freak. No matter how many creatures I came across, none were like me. I was the unicorn of the supernatural world.

That man knew something about me. Enough to hunt me down. While my momma lay burning on the floor of my childhood home, he'd stepped over her and reached for me.

"You've blamed yourself for your momma's death for far too long, child," Susan whispered. "It's time to let that burden go."

"I will," I said. "I need to know why."

"What if he doesn't give you the answers you're looking for?"

"He will," I said.

"You seem so sure of that."

I could no longer look her in the eye. "It's best you not know."

"Yes." She sighed. "I suppose you're right."

"I will come home someday."

Susan smiled. "I know you will. When you're ready. You gotta find your peace first, Ember. It's there waitin' on you. You'll find it when the time is right."

We sat in silence for several minutes, listening to the rain pattering the window behind her. Judging by the dim lighting in the rooms across from me, it was nighttime.

"What day is it?" I asked.

16

"It's after midnight, so I guess it's Friday now. You've been asleep for three full days." Susan glanced at the nurses' station, visible through the sliding glass door to my room. "The doctors couldn't figure you out. Your wounds were healing, but your brain didn't want to work quite right. I told them when I arrived to give you a little time. I knew you'd come around when you were ready."

The memory of the scorched bird on the alley wall and Fluffy's pile of dust flashed before my eyes. My breathing hitched, but I said nothing. That's not something I could share.

"I'm assuming now that you're awake, you've got your brain all sorted out."

I nodded, though I wasn't sure that was entirely true until those pain pills wore off.

"Well, good. That's very good." She patted my hand again. "Your brothers and sisters send their love, of course."

We both knew that was a lie. Back home, I had three brothers and four sisters of various ages who lived with me. All were foster care rejects that Susan took in. No matter how many candles they had on their birthday cakes, they were smart enough to avoid me.

While living in the small town of Eufaula, Alabama, I'd had my fair share of unkind words spoken about me. Freak. Hooligan. Pyro. Most of them started by my own foster kin. I'll admit they were pretty much justified by my actions. The police might not have been rocket scientists, but they were hardworking and smart enough to keep an eye on me. The trouble was I didn't stick around long. I bounced from city to city, following leads. Most of them never panned out, and I'd come home to rest for a while.

Twisting my wrists to test the tension on my restraints, I noticed Susan watching me. "You don't have to stick around for this part."

She smiled. "Afraid I'll rat you out to the police once you're gone?"

I stopped. "Of course not. I just don't want my life to keep tossing junk at you. You shouldn't have to lie for me, Sue. Heck, you shouldn't have to do any of this."

"Mind that tongue or I'll mind it for you, young lady," she scolded. Even though heck wasn't really a swear word, Sue thought it was ill-fitting for a lady. She was the only reason I never swore. I respected her too much.

I couldn't help but smile at her stern look. Or the way she tried to

17

press out the wrinkles in my hospital gown. It felt good to be mothered. I'd missed that while I'd been on the road. "And don't you be worrying about me none. I know how to handle myself."

"That I don't doubt."

She leaned in and kissed me on the forehead. "Promise me you'll be safe."

"I'll try." That was the best I could offer.

She rose, patted me on the head, and moved toward the door. Before it closed behind her, she was already working her charm on the cop. No one could resist a cup of hot coffee from a sweet southern lady like her.

The instant the cop's attention shifted, I focused on my wrists. The tingling came a split second before smoke rose from my restraints. I had to focus to keep the flame minimal or I'd risk setting off the fire alarm.

Ridding myself of my IV, I leaped out of bed and tore open the closet in search of my clothes. They hung in a small blue plastic bag and stank of Fluffy's urine and smoke. I scrunched up my nose as I put them on. Urine was better than letting my butt hang out as I escaped the hospital. I'd find somewhere to wash later.

As soon as I snapped the final boot buckle in place, I headed for the door. The cop was leaning against the wall now for support. His eyes looked heavy.

Focusing my attention on the glass door, I created a small beam of heat to melt a hole in the glass. The instant I was through, I shoved the heat toward the nurse's station. A computer burst into flames, sending two nurses into a flutter. Papers flew into the air as they tossed their charts and hurried for a fire extinguisher.

Laughing to myself, I redirected the heat to another patient's closed curtain. The fibers lit and smoke began to billow out into the hall.

"Fire!" the cop yelled and raced to pull the alarm.

Patients woke all around the ward. Nurses shouted as they worked to put out the fire. Patients performed an awkward IV pole shuffle as they fled. Susan grinned. She shot me a thumbs up from where she stood at the instant coffee machine.

She called out, and I turned to see a small wad of cash flying through the air. I grabbed it and shoved it deep into my pocket.

"Don't you be skipping any meals, you hear?"

"Yes, ma'am." I waved goodbye.

My heavy footfalls echoed in the vacant stairwell. On the first floor, I slipped into a supply closet when the fire trucks rolled into the hospital lot. Several masked men rushed by. Before the sliding doors closed, I was on the move.

Never before had it felt so freeing to escape. For the first time, I had Susan's permission. That helped lighten the guilt load. But knowing the man I'd hunted for so long was nearby made every sacrifice worth it.

I would find him, no matter what it took. He was going to pay.

CHAPTER 4

*W*hile some girls wasted their teen years chasing boys, I perfected a few life skills. Like hot-wiring a car. I'd lost count of how many times that came in handy. Susan had insisted that my momma's dream of a good education not die with her. So I'd gone to school like she asked. But showing up and sticking around were two very different things.

Slipping behind the wheel of a Jeep, I worked fast to shut off the alarm. Sweet silence filled the air. The needle showed three-quarters of a tank of gas. Luck was finally smiling on me.

Crime scene tape roped off the alley when I arrived. I rolled past and parallel parked a few cars away. Pieces of government equipment remained behind.

"I guess they can't find the source of their gas leak," I muttered.

Keeping my head ducked low, I hurried to reach my hiding spot. I grabbed my stashed bag and did a quick check to make sure everything was safe. Even with the scent of day-old trash clinging to its fabric, it still smelled better than I did.

I searched a several-block radius from the condo to locate a place to get cleaned up. Slipping inside the Greedy Hamster, I passed a frazzled bartender. There was little space to move during the booming lunch rush.

With the bathroom lock engaged, I washed in record time. The water turned grimy as smoke and wolf urine leached out of my clothes. I made an attempt to use the hand dryer on them, but a pounding at the door told me time was up.

A tray of steaming food caught my eye as I passed the kitchen. I gave in to the temptation to steal a fry. The mixture of grease and salt told me it'd been far too long since I ate.

But the small wad of cash in my pocket had to last.

Back at the Jeep, I sunk low in my seat, determined to watch the street. Cars rolled by at regular intervals. Couples with small children came and went from the condo, headed for the park at the end of the road. The doorman directed a delivery van to the rear of the building.

It was business as usual. All apart from one important detail: a Rolls Royce sat parked in front. Its silver paint gleamed in the sunlight. I would have bet the interior still had that new-car smell. Judging by the other cars parked in this neighborhood, the Rolls was a rarity.

Cars didn't do anything for me. One man's priceless baby was another man's target of mayhem. I wasn't interested in the underbelly of Denver. Not the human side, at least.

What did interest me was how fast that car was replaced. Only someone with a great deal of money and connections could pull that off. I doubted there were many dealers in the area.

I didn't know for sure that it belonged to my momma's killer, but my gut told me to follow that car. I'd learned to listen to my instincts. Sure, there was that one time that it led me to a nest of hungry vampires, but I was a silver lining kind of gal. I lived. That was good enough for me.

Ripples of heat rose from the hood of the Jeep. June was a nightmare no matter where you lived. Growing up in the Deep South taught me to deal with high humidity and bugs the size of Frisbees. Denver had nothing on Savannah or Alabama.

I ignored the growling in my stomach and moved to the back seat. That helped minimize my exposure to the sun. Even with the windows cracked, I panted like a freakin' dog.

Not long after school buses took to the streets, a cop car rolled to a stop at the alleyway. I peered between the seats. One of the men was from the hospital that morning.

I'm so busted.

If there was one thing I'd learned, it was that paranoia kept you alive and out of jail. Digging through the cargo area in search of a cover, I groaned.

"Of course my luck would dive straight into Crapsville." I lifted a wool blanket and glared at its offensive texture. "Talk about a sweatbox from hell."

The cops hung around long enough for me to turn into a puddle of sweat. The instant they pulled away from the curb, I burst free. Pressing my face to the window, I sucked in great gulps of cooler air.

I allowed myself small breaks outside of the car as the afternoon turned to dusk. The Rolls didn't move. No one came to check out the crime scene. I watched to see if any of the fight-club crowd would return. Some were sure to be nosy. The explosion had been all over the news. It wouldn't surprise me if Fuzzbert showed up to find any cash he'd stashed away.

When the last threads of light bled from the sky, I couldn't deny my stomach any longer. I snagged a hot dog from a food truck. The remaining sixty-eight dollars wouldn't get me far, but I'd stretch every penny of it.

The rumbling in my stomach abated, and a new weariness set in. I'd spent a good part of my day trying to heal. Resting in the back of a sweltering car wasn't as easy as it sounded, but it helped restore a bit of my energy. Enough to seal my final wounds, at least. The bruises would take time.

Pressing into the headrest, I fought against sleep. I was a night owl by default, which came in handy when hunting state to state. I bummed rides off more truck drivers than I cared to count. Most of them were nice. The others earned their missing fingers for trying to mess with me.

My eyes grew heavy as the cooler night breeze slipped through the narrow gap of my window. I was nodding off when the doorman's voice called from across the street, "Let me get that door for you, sir."

Popping my head up, I saw my momma's killer slide behind the driver's seat of the Rolls Royce. The doorman tried to close the door for him, but it yanked right out of his hands. No tip was given.

"So you're a cheap bastard, too," I said.

I tapped the wires together, and the Jeep roared to life. I eased out of my spot and followed the Rolls. By the time we hit the edge of Denver, it was full blown night. That black-eyed bastard spent an hour guiding me on a tour of a suburban nightmare.

"Looks like I'm not the only one who's paranoid," I said, easing behind an older model SUV.

He wasn't my first mark. I knew to keep my distance and blend with what little traffic there was. Off-roading vehicles were a dime a dozen in this state. I wouldn't stand out.

Entering the interstate six cars behind him, I kept my pace slower than his. At times, I allowed the distance to reach half a mile. I eyed each exit to make sure he didn't take a sudden turn. Instead, he seemed quite content to cruise at only five miles over the speed limit. Wherever he was going, he was in no hurry to arrive.

He pulled over for gas one time. I eased the Jeep into a station across the street. Keeping him in my sights, I put a few gallons into my own tank in case he decided to take off across the country. I wasn't about to lose him because I was a poor planner.

The farther we drove from Denver, the more distance there was between exits. From time to time, I spied the glow of a town against the cloudy sky. The mountains grew more impressive as we headed south on state highways. I blasted the AC almost as high as I did the speakers. Belting out eighties rock helped me stay awake.

Half an hour later, the Rolls took a side road. A quick glance at my phone's GPS showed nothing in that direction. No town. No rest stop. Nothing but uninhabited mountains. At least, I hoped they were uninhabited. Who knew what creatures lurked in the dark out here?

"Where are you going?" I eased the Jeep off the highway.

With the traffic almost nonexistent now, I had to maintain a greater distance. Coming out of one bend, I saw the Rolls drifting into another. With each turn, the gradient increased. Stress wound me tighter than a jack-in-the-box. It would be easy for me to lose him up here.

My headlights didn't feel powerful enough to cut through the inky night. I spotted eyes shining from the woods, but passed by too fast to get a second glance.

"It could be anything," I said. "A harmless coyote. Doesn't mean it has to be something supernatural."

The clouds parted, and for a moment, the forest shimmered with moonglow. The dappled light filtered through tall pines, firs, and aspens. But in the thickest parts, it enhanced the eerie darkness.

I laughed. "Maybe I need to tone down the paranoia a bit."

But the farther I drove, the more I felt like I was being watched. Hairs rose on the back of my neck. I kept a close watch on my rearview mirror, sure that something darted across the road behind me.

As I turned a sharp bend, the light of the moon vanished. A dark shape flew over the hood of the car, and I slammed on the brakes. The tires skidded, and the Jeep fishtailed. The brakes locked down and sent me careening toward the guardrail. I closed my eyes and threw up my hands to protect my face. Sparks and the grinding of metal filled my world.

Then an ear-piercing screech filled the car. My eardrums vibrated as the car tipped.

I'm going over!

Inches above my head, great talons pierced the roof. I cried out as the car lifted into the air and then dropped back onto all four tires. The shock absorbers took the brunt of the impact. The chassis groaned. The car fell still.

My hands shook as I peeled them off the steering wheel. "What was that?"

With a powerful flap of its wings, a bird appeared from the valley below. It climbed into the sky with impossible speed. I leaned hard enough against the steering wheel to earn a new bruise come morning.

"The wingspan has to be at least thirty feet," I whispered. I used my hand to try to measure it against the distant road. "That thing could carry off a baby elephant."

Or a car. I shuddered at the thought.

The bird soared on the wind with a grace that betrayed its enormous size. Distinct color variations in its feathers appeared in the moonlight. The patterns reminded me of an eagle, but far more intricate.

The bird was mesmerizing to watch as it dipped toward the tree line. Then it burst back up into the air with terrific speed. Each flap of its wings bowed the trees toward the ground with a force to match that of a small cyclone.

I knew that I needed to go. I'd already let far too much distance come between us. But I couldn't make myself move.

There was something about this bird that called to me. Though the creature had sent me into a panic, it had also saved me from falling into the ravine. What sort of intelligence did it have? What did it feel like to command the skies?

For several minutes, the bird circled. It appeared to have no destination in mind. Nothing else moved. No sounds, apart from the life-changing guitar riffs of Metallica, disturbed the peace. Then, just as suddenly as it had arrived, the bird was gone. I craned my neck to search the skies, but the bird never reappeared.

"Beautiful," I whispered. That one word summed up so much, and yet it didn't feel large enough to capture what I was feeling.

After one last look at the vacant skies, I pulled the Jeep back onto the road. The ride was not so smooth. The tires pulled a bit to the right. But when I gunned the engine, it followed my command.

"Where are you?" I said.

By now, the man I pursued could've disappeared completely. After several miles, I noticed a distinct downward slope to the road. The turns became sharper, the dropoff more perilous. Near the bottom of the mountain was a pair of headlights.

"That'd better be you." I urged the speedometer on.

Several miles separated us now. No matter how hard I gunned the engine, I couldn't catch up. With each sharp bend, I had to slam on my brakes or risk flying off the edge. The night's shadows stretched on, making it harder to judge distance. It took a half hour before I reached the bottom. I white-knuckled the wheel as I blew by a babbling stream alongside a straight but narrow road. The stream grew into a river, fed by the melting snow of the mountains.

Lights appeared up ahead, and I eased off the gas pedal.

"Havenwood Falls," I read aloud as I passed the sign. Glancing at my GPS again, I saw nothing. No town name. No road apart from this one. "Well, that's not weird at all."

As I drove over the town limit, warmth seeped into my chest. It was like what I felt while watching the bird. There were no words to describe it. It was more of a feeling of coming home. Which was absurd, since I didn't actually remember what home felt like.

Ignoring the speed limit, I passed a high school on my left, a turnoff for a ski resort on my right. Street signs with ascending numbers caught my eye before the town center came into view. It looked quaint. There was an array of boutique shops, a couple coffee houses, consignment shops, and more. There was even a cute little gazebo next to a fountain. It was the sort of place where good things happened to nice people.

A large banner with the words "Midsummer Night's Festival" hung across Main Street. Large posters with a Shakespearean feel were hung in several of the windows.

"Wow. I really don't belong around here," I said. Rolling down my window, I breathed in deep the clean mountain air. "But it's not a half bad place to rest up."

Havenwood Falls was larger than I would've imagined when entering the town. I searched for the missing Rolls for an hour, but it had disappeared. I checked out the cemetery and drove through a development with a country club, searching driveways for the missing car. I spotted several motorcycles parked out front of a building named Swords of the Infernal Night, according to the sign over the door. SIN for short—that seemed appropriate.

"Cute name," I chuckled as I passed the Get Buffed! business sign. Not that I would ever step foot in a place like that. Sweaty men ogling themselves in the mirror while they pumped iron wasn't my thing.

"That bites," I grumbled, admitting defeat. He was gone.

There was no sign of taillights on the road leading away from Havenwood Falls. I visually searched the mountainsides for several minutes to be sure. Convinced that he remained in town, at least for the night, I made my way back to the big park with a sign that said Danzan Park. Snatching my bag off the back seat, I found a community bathroom. It surprised me when the door swung open.

"Well, look at that." I locked the door behind me. "I didn't even have to pick the lock. People around here must be way too trusting."

With my shirt hung over the sink, I stared at myself in the mirror. Every way I turned, my flesh showed a patchwork of nasty bruises. The one over Fluffy's last bite was an angry purple.

I dabbed cool paper towels over the bruises. I cleaned away the sweat. I'd lost count of how many times I'd done a strip wash like this one. Teenagers should be at home, draining every drop of hot water from their parents' tank. Not standing in some strange bleached public restroom.

My hip bones pressed against the skin. My cheeks looked less plump than when I had lived back home, getting three square meals a day. The loss of body fat gave me a six-pack, though.

"It's worth it." Leaning over the sink, I splashed water on my face. "I found him."

The water ran between the layers of scar tissue that covered the right side of my face. I stared at my burns without emotion. The burns were a part of me, whether I liked it or not. My momma died the night I got these. Walking away with a few scars seemed a small price to pay for my life. Losing my momma . . . well, that was just about the most any gal could pay.

Of all the wounds I'd survived and healed, my tears were helpless to reverse this damage.

Standing there under the blinking halogen lights, I poked at the wounded flesh. The skin was puffy and pale. It never tanned like the rest of me.

"What do you care how it looks?" I asked my reflection. "You're never around long enough to hook up with a guy."

Wasn't that the truth?

There was a time my burns were an embarrassment. People stopped and stared. Kids were cruel. But every snide remark made me stronger. They were a daily reminder of my purpose.

With a sigh, I braided my tangled hair and donned my clothes again. The leather pants were a pain to pull on with my skin still damp. I could probably get another day or two out of this set, as long as I didn't get into any more fights.

Once back at the Jeep, I made one more drive around town just to be sure, then turned the car toward the town center. Waking up in front of the police station in a stolen car didn't seem like the smartest idea, so I made my way to the southern side of the square.

Pulling into a parking spot in front of Coffee Haven, a hipster sort of coffee shop that looked way too trendy for my liking, I turned off the engine. Despite the quick wash I had earlier in the day, I needed to inspect my wounds again. I reclined the driver's seat and searched the sky through the sunroof one last time. Clouds concealed the moon, and a light mist had begun to fall. I turned onto my side and sighed. Sleeping in cars had never been my forte, but there was no other option. My measly stash of cash wasn't enough to cover even one night at that cute little inn at the end of the block.

Balling the blanket into a pillow, I closed my eyes. "You escaped me tonight. I won't let you get away a second time."

CHAPTER 5

*M*ornings sucked. So did the people who loved them. I hated all those perky smiles and chipper greetings, as if six a.m. was the best freakin' time of the day. News flash, folks. The rest of the world dragged until someone took pity on them and passed an espresso.

Teenagers didn't do mornings. Period. Since I was still nineteen for another two days, I considered myself an expert on all things moody, melodramatic, and insomniac. So when a pounding on my car window sent me into panic mode the next morning, I came up fighting.

"What the heck, man?" A spike of heat flared in my palms, scorching the bottom of the steering wheel. I snuffed out the flames and hoped the guy didn't notice the small puff of smoke.

His shadow fell over me when he stepped up to the window. It relieved my temporary state of sun blindness long enough to reveal that I'd sworn at a cop. Or rather, a rent-a-cop, by the looks of it.

"Perfect." I rubbed my hands over my face. This was not how I wanted the day to begin. Especially since I was sitting in a stolen car.

"Ma'am, are you aware that you're in a no parking zone?"

I blinked. It was hard to focus with a massive crick in my neck and a hole in my stomach the size of the Grand Canyon. It took me a full minute to process that he wasn't accusing me of falling asleep in someone else's car.

See? I could find the silver lining even at the butt crack of dawn.

"This isn't a handicapped space," I called back through the gap at the top of my window.

The shiny gold letters on his badge told me his name was Lloyd. He turned and pointed at a paper sign stapled to a wooden stake at the front of my car. I couldn't read the words, as the sides folded in on themselves in the wind, but I got the gist of it. I was in a temporary unloading zone for some stupid town festival.

That's when I remembered the festival signs and groaned. Some days I had the worst luck.

"I'm going to have to ask you to vacate the premises." He placed one hand on his hip, and with the other, he jerked his thumb back over his shoulder.

Lloyd looked determined to stand right there and watch until I moved. This posed a slight problem, considering I had to hotwire my ride.

"Can't you give a girl a second to wake up?" I yawned and stretched my arms as high as the ceiling of the Jeep would allow.

The young man pursed his lips in response.

He didn't look much older than me. Mid-twenties at the most. The closer I looked, the more I began to suspect that he was a greenie. He definitely wasn't a real cop. Probably just hired on a part-time basis when the real cops were too busy to deal with the small stuff. His shirt was wrinkle-free and the seams of his pants were pressed. His badge didn't have a scratch on it. The holster at his hip was still shiny with polish.

I could take him if I wanted to.

"I'm afraid you're going to have to finish waking up somewhere else, ma'am." His voice even cracked a little as he tried to sound official. "The vendors will be setting up shortly, and I have to clear the area."

I turned to look out the passenger window. Main Street and the park across from it looked empty. Not a single soul, vendor table, or vehicle was in sight.

"The place is a ghost town. Looks like you can spare me five minutes."

Lloyd's jaw flinched. From the corner of my eye, I saw his hand travel to rest on his Taser.

"Exit the vehicle, ma'am."

My hands tightened on the bottom of the steering wheel, concealing the burn marks. If he called me ma'am one more time . . .

"Now." He backed away three steps so I could open my door. I paused to consider my options.

I could do as he said and let him puff up with self-importance. Then he would threaten me with a ticket that I would never pay.

I could take him out. That option sounded pretty good right about now.

Or I could sit right here and see how far he would take this.

When he grabbed the Taser, I sighed and reached for the door handle.

Might as well play along. I couldn't get run out of town before I found my momma's killer.

"I'm coming. I'm coming." The Jeep door creaked as it swung open.

I arched my back to ease the stiffness as I stood. Everything ached. On top of that, I looked like a mess. After a night of tossing and turning, my braid was ruined. A wild mane of fire surrounded my face. When the wind changed directions, it revealed my burns.

He gave me a once-over. "That's quite a scar you've got there."

"I could say the same about your crater face, but I'm not rude." I gritted my teeth. I sure would have loved to punch him in the throat right about now.

As a child, I was a sweet little thing. I'd spend my weekends picking flowers and making necklaces with them for my momma. I baked cookies and made sweet tea. I smiled a lot back then, too. Even had proper manners.

Now I had a chip on my shoulder. One that I usually didn't stick around long enough to apologize for.

Lloyd narrowed his gaze. "You a runaway or something?"

"That's none of your business. I'm an adult. End of story." This guy was tap dancing all over my rising bad temper.

Thin lines appeared around his eyes when he squinted against the sunlight. I snorted. The rookie hadn't even earned sunglass marks on the sides of his face yet.

"Step aside."

"Excuse me?" I crossed my arms over my chest. This guy was starting to piss me off. I had to work to control the tingling in my hands.

"I said, step aside."

"Not going to happen." I stood my ground. I'd had about all I was going to take from him.

His eyes widened. Apparently, he'd never been told no by a suspect before. Or whatever the heck he thought I was. "No?"

"You have no probable cause or evidence of criminal activity against me to give you the right to search my car. Judging by your attire, I'd say you aren't even a real cop. I happen to know that if you are nothing more than private security, you have about as much authority as I do right now. So the answer is no. You do not have my permission. In fact, you have the complete opposite."

Lloyd wiped at a bead of sweat on his brow. He looked baffled.

"And furthermore," I took a small step toward him and smiled when he flinched. "I don't appreciate you treating me like a common criminal. Sleeping in my car is legal. I was not parked in the wrong spot, and that sign was not there last night."

Looking toward the sidewalk, I spotted a mallet, wooden stakes, a stack of signs, and a staple gun.

"It is my job to—"

"Yeah, I get it, Barney Fife. You've got a duty. Don't we all. But you need to learn some people skills, or you'll wind up on the wrong end of that Taser one of these days."

His finger flinched against the Taser. "Is that a threat?"

"Of course not." My words dripped with poison-laced honey. "I'd call it friendly advice."

He shuffled his feet, seeming unsure of what to do next. When he scratched the back of his neck, I almost burst out laughing. This guy was a real piece of work. If the real law enforcement in the area was anything like Lloyd, I didn't have anything to worry about.

A sudden blast of a car horn startled me. I looked over my shoulder, but not before seeing Lloyd rush to put his Taser away.

A sleek sedan paused at the street corner before turning our way.

"Is there a problem here?" a smooth voice called from within the darkened interior.

The windows were as black as the paint job. I couldn't imagine that was legal, but one look at Lloyd told me that he'd be the last person to say anything about it. The driver kept his face in the shadow of the vehicle.

"What's it to you?" I asked.

The vehicle was not a marked police car. In fact, I couldn't see any visible form of identification on the vehicle from where I stood.

"I'm a concerned citizen. Nothing more."

"How sweet, but I can take care of myself."

"Yes," the man drew out the word like the hiss of a snake. "I can see that. Seems to me that Lloyd here might not understand that quite as well as I do."

The rent-a-cop straightened his shoulders. "I have orders to clear the area, Mr. Laroc. What with the festival and all happening today."

Unlike Lloyd, I didn't cower back from the hard once-over that came from the blacked-out car. The man turned his attention back to me. From the depths of the darkness, I caught the glint of a golden eyeshine.

"You're new to Havenwood Falls. I haven't seen you around town before."

I shrugged. "Arrived last night."

A string of smoke escaped through the open window. "Are you here for work or pleasure?"

"I don't see how that's your business."

"A girl who sleeps in her car doesn't seem all that keen on sticking around long. It is my business if you intend to stir up any trouble."

Well, now that was interesting. This concerned citizen had a reason for nosing around and wanted to be sure I knew it. I made a show of wiping my nose so that I could conceal my inhale. I caught the scent of a vampire and the foul stench of an ogre. But there was a strange odor in the air. One that I couldn't place.

"A bit of both, then." With another shrug, I leaned back against the Jeep. This conversation needed to end.

The engine of the car gave a sudden throaty roar. I tried to see into the interior, but it was almost as if a veil of night lay between me and the driver. I recognized it as a glamour requiring a mage to be present. That must have been the final person in the vehicle.

Whoever this guy was, he didn't want to be seen.

The hairs on my arm began to rise. My gut clenched as I fisted my hands at my side. Something wasn't right. The only time I ever saw a blending of species like this was at a fight. Or in the underbelly of some criminal organization. Havenwood Falls hardly seemed the place to find a crime boss. But if my momma's killer was hiding out here, then I was dead wrong. The peaceful little rural town could be a front for something far more sinister.

What other evil lurked within these town limits?

Turning to glance at Lloyd, I knew right off that he was human. No supernatural could be that big of a bumbling idiot.

"Well, I'm sure Lloyd here will be happy to let you off with a warning. After he collects a few minor details for his records, of course." The man's voice was as smooth as a razor's edge now. "I'm sure you understand."

I had zero intention of handing over a single ounce of detail about myself.

"Isn't that right, Lloyd?" Another puff of smoke exited the car. This time I realized it didn't have the scent of a cigarette or cigar. Instead, it smelled of brimstone.

My stomach clenched. Was the driver a demon of some sort? Or perhaps a dragon shifter phasing in and out of his form?

Lloyd stood to attention, breaking into my thoughts. "Yes, sir! I won't let you down, Mr. Laroc. You can count on me."

I rolled my eyes. What a pansy.

"As for you, missy, I'd be careful of that tongue while you're staying in Havenwood Falls. Folks around here don't take kindly to veiled snide remarks. Especially from outsiders."

A smirk tugged at my lips. "Who said I was trying to veil them?"

A deep chuckle emerged from the car before the window rose and the sedan rolled away. Lloyd breathed out a sigh of relief from behind me. Whoever that man was, he held some power in this town. Or at least over Lloyd.

"You always wet yourself around that guy?" I asked.

Lloyd blinked and then refocused on me. I was actually impressed when his boyish features settled into a scowl. "You don't know what you're talking about. Mr. Laroc is an important man."

I pushed off from the car. "Whatever. I know fear when I smell it."

He stiffened. "Did you say smell?"

"Yeah. Smell." I laughed and turned back to slide into the driver's seat. "You'll figure it out someday."

And that was it. No threats of a ticket. No additional warning or huffing from Lloyd. After I slammed the Jeep door shut, I looked back to see Lloyd staring down the street.

That guy really messed with his head.

Lloyd hesitated before moving to collect his signpost items from the sidewalk. With his back turned, I connected the wires. The Jeep thrummed to life, and I threw the car into reverse.

"Watch out!"

After years of training for the unexplained, I'd developed lightning fast reflexes. They didn't save me this time. One push on the gas pedal and I ran into something. The car rocked as I slammed on the brakes.

"Crap." Throwing open my door, I raced around the back to find a man sprawled on the ground. It looked like he'd been clipped and spun clean around.

"Oh, my god. You killed him!" I looked up to see horror written all over Lloyd's face. "We're dead. We're so, so dead."

The urge to punch his ugly pockmarked nose rose up again. "He's not dead. He just got knocked out when he landed."

Lloyd looked between me and the man with such utter disbelief that I almost chuckled. Who would hire a guy like him to be weekend security?

"That's going to hurt in the morning." The fallen man groaned and rolled onto his back.

Smudges marred the front of his shirt. The fabric showed a few tears. Minor road rash markings littered one side of his face where his five o'clock stubble ended. Other than that, he looked fine.

Scratch that. He was way better than fine. His hair was a sandy blond, with fascinating streaks of white. The coloring was a stark contrast to the warm tawny eyes that stared up at me. Though I was sure he was the sort of guy that girls would do a double-take for, I didn't get the sense that he was cocky.

"Well, hello to you, too." He smiled, interrupting my assessment.

I snorted. Maybe a little cocky.

Lloyd spluttered when the man pushed up to his feet, shoved the cop aside and offered me his hand. "The name's Atticus, and you're welcome to run me over any day you like."

Calluses lined the palm of his hand. His skin was kissed by the sun. I guessed him to be some sort of day laborer, judging by the sheer size of him. The telltale angle of a once-broken nose, paired with his lopsided grin, made him look younger than he probably was.

"That's quite a grip you've got there," I said when he continued shaking my hand. "I'm impressed."

He beamed back at me.

That smile could do bad things to me.

Atticus was hot. That might not be the manliest sentiment, but it was true nonetheless. Right down to his flannel shirt, dusty work boots, and the large scar that peeked out of his rolled sleeves.

If I'd known guys like him lived in Colorado, I'd have come out this way sooner.

Lloyd waved a hand in front of Atticus's face. "Are you feeling okay? Any concussion? Head trauma is completely common in hit-and-runs."

"I didn't run." I rolled my eyes. "I'm standing right here."

"Go away, Lloyd," Atticus said.

"Go away? Well, I never." The cop bristled. "Are you pressing charges against this girl, Mr. Laroc? I can call the sheriff to write her up right here and now, if you'd like. I saw it all. She was definitely at fault."

"Go away," Atticus and I said at the same time.

Lloyd's ears went red. His hands fluttered around him, unsure of what to do. Finally, he threw them in the air and walked away.

"Is he always like that?" I asked, watching the rent-a-cop fumble with his armful of materials. He dropped a few, tried to balance them on the top of his foot, and then gave up trying.

"Yeah. Rumor has it his mom dropped him a few times on his head. I prefer to think he was hexed."

"Did you say hexed? As in voodoo or witchcraft?"

Atticus's wink told me that he was joking. Thank god for that. I'd run into my fair share of witches, and some of them were as mean as rattlesnakes.

"Why'd he call you Mr. Laroc?"

"Well, that is my name. But I assume you're thinking about my uncle. I thought I saw his car pull away when I rounded the corner." He sighed. "I hope he wasn't rude. My uncle can be a bit abrupt at times."

That's an understatement.

"It's fine," I said instead. "He was just making sure Lloyd wasn't harassing me."

"Right. He's thoughtful like that." But the furrow of Atticus's brow deepened.

Not wanting to get dragged into a family affair, I glanced at the small dent in the back of the Jeep and winced. "Sorry about taking you out like that. You came out of nowhere."

Atticus waved me off. "It was my fault. I heard raised voices and came over to snoop. Guess I was standing a bit too close."

It was almost refreshing how open he was about his attempts to eavesdrop. I'd have done the same thing. Curiosity killed the cat . . . or ran him over with an SUV.

"Are you okay?" This time I took my time looking him over. For medical purposes, of course. He was a good sport and turned to give me the full view.

"Sure thing. A few bumps and scrapes. Nothing I can't handle."

Now that he mentioned a bump, I noticed a nasty one starting to form on his forehead. The split skin leaked a small trickle of blood spreading into his eyebrow.

"You'll need to get that looked at." I motioned to his head.

His fingertips were painted with blood when he pulled them away from the bump. "I'm a fast healer."

I didn't doubt that. I could sense that he wasn't human. Not by a long shot. But his scent—it was foreign to me, and yet somehow familiar. Like a lost word teetering on the tip of my tongue, but held out of reach.

"Right. Well, I should probably—" I hiked my finger over my shoulder at the open driver's side door. "I'm parked in the wrong spot on the wrong day."

Atticus glanced at Lloyd, who had moved to post another sign. "Yeah. Havenwood Falls may be small, but our festivals are mighty. It can get kind of hectic."

I laughed. I couldn't imagine anything about this sleepy little town being hectic.

"It was nice running into you." I started toward the car but fell still when his hand brushed my arm. I had a thing about people touching me, but I gave him the benefit of the doubt before I took him out.

"Do you like food?"

"Food?" I smirked.

Atticus rubbed at the back of his neck and shrugged. "Yeah, you know. The stuff that takes care of that obnoxious growling your stomach is doing right now."

Mortified, I pressed a hand to my stomach. He was right. I'd been too preoccupied to notice that my hunger level had reached DEFCON 1.

"There's a place I know that serves the best waffles in town. My treat."

I shot him a suspicious glance. "Waffles?"

"I get that it's kind of weird to share a waffle with a guy you just hit with your car, but when you stop and think about it, you owe me."

"I owe you?" I laughed. Wow. He had some balls to go with those muscles. "How do you figure that?"

"Well, you see there's this thing . . ." He pretended to think it over. "Yeah. I've got nothing. I just want to talk to you a bit longer."

The laugh lines around his eyes told me that he liked to have a good time. His smile was sincere. His eyes were clear of any visible hidden agendas. Atticus looked like a good old boy. Which made it hard to place him with the nosy guy from the sedan. Atticus didn't have any of his uncle's creep vibes, but he might know something worth hearing.

"Thanks for the offer, but I—"

"One waffle, that's all I'm asking for. Then I promise I'm out of your life, if you want."

If I want . . . oh, boy. That could easily turn into the loaded question of my day.

I could imagine a great many things I'd like to do with Atticus Laroc, but none of them brought me any closer to finding my momma's killer. So I glanced back at the idling Jeep. Atticus was a distraction—one that I wouldn't mind entertaining on any other day, but I had plans.

"You're new here, right?" he hurried to add when he realized he was losing me. "I know what it's like to be in a new place. No friends. No family. I get it."

"Who said I'm alone?" Atticus glanced at the lone backpack in the passenger seat of the car. He'd spotted my blanket as well. I sighed. "Fine. You caught me. I'm passing through."

He tilted his head to the side, pursing his lips to give me a hard stare. "Nobody *passes through* this town. It's not exactly on the way to anywhere."

"Right?" I nodded. "What's the deal with this place, anyway?"

Atticus took a step toward me. "An answer for a waffle. That's the deal."

Oh, he was good. And I was starving. Plus he was a local with obvious connections.

Am I really agreeing to this?

Pushing my hair back out of my face, I waited as his gaze flitted over my scars. There was no look of disgust or horror. His smile didn't fade an ounce. Maybe he really was a nice guy.

It wouldn't kill me to give him one meal in exchange for information.

"Make it a chocolate chip waffle and I'm in."

CHAPTER 6

One bite into my triple layer chocolate waffle told me that I'd never truly lived before. It melted in my mouth and made me think of sinful things. Atticus slumped into his chair, arm slung over the back, and gave me a knowing smile.

"It's a good thing we didn't put a bet on these." I wiped a dab of chocolate off my chin.

Atticus grinned and shoved a tall glass of milk my way. "Trust me, you're going to need this, too."

I wasn't much of a milk drinker. In fact, I wasn't much on anything that even resembled health food. Give me a bag of chips and a candy bar and I was set. But, yet again, he knew what he was talking about. The milk washed down the chocolatey goodness with perfection.

"All right. I'll admit it. These are the best waffles I've ever had." I sat back to give my stomach a chance to expand so I could shovel in a bit more. "Double brownie points for the location, too."

Atticus had brought me to the country club for breakfast. The interior looked like a log cabin fit for an HGTV show. There was a beautiful stone fireplace, with a woman perched on the hearth playing an acoustic guitar. Two plush couches sat a few feet away so that during the winter months you could snuggle by a roaring fire. The bar, brightly colored with hundreds of bottles seated on glass shelves, stood off to my left.

Lifting my face, I stared up at the huge chandelier overhead. Electric candles sat unlit under hurricane glass. Floor to ceiling windows stood no less than thirty feet high and spanned the entire far wall. Not even I could deny the beauty of an early morning overlooking a golf course. From where I sat, I could see a team of greenskeepers trimming the fairways. One man bent low to check on the sprinklers. The water hung like a fine mist in the air, giving this place an almost magical feel.

"So you want to tell me why you're in my town?" Atticus asked.

Digging into my waffles again so I didn't have to give him a full answer, I shrugged. "No real reason."

"That line might have worked on Lloyd, but I'm not such an easy sell. I know you're in trouble."

My knife clattered to the plate, making me jump. A couple at a table nearby glanced our way.

"I'm not trying to out you. Heck, I don't even know your name yet." Atticus leaned closer. "But I can tell that you're in a bad way, and I want to help."

"Why?" My defenses kicked in.

He seemed almost hurt by the question. "Because I'm a nice guy."

I snorted and picked up my knife. Even though it was nothing more than a butter knife, it felt good to have it in my hand. I missed my dagger. Fuzzbert must have run off with it during the chaos.

Stupid troll. I saw him eyeing it before my fight with Fluffy.

"Nice guys don't get far in this world," I said.

He cocked his head. "That may be true in some towns. But Havenwood Falls isn't like other places."

Though I was only halfway through my waffles, I sat back and pushed the plate aside. Not so far that I couldn't sneak another forkful or two if I chose, mind you.

"Fine. I'll bite. What makes this place so different?"

Atticus placed his palms on the table and smoothed out the tablecloth. When he spoke, it was in a hushed tone. I got the distinct feeling he didn't want anyone else to hear our conversation. "Do you believe in ghosts?"

I stared at him for a moment before I burst out laughing. "The town's haunted? Is that it?"

"Shh." He motioned for me to lower my voice. "No. But also yes at the same time."

I stopped laughing when I saw that his smile had faded. "Wait. You're serious?"

"Havenwood Falls is special." He glanced around. I followed his gaze and saw that no one was paying any attention to us. I was starting to get a vibe about this place, but I focused on Atticus instead. "There's an energy here that draws certain people to it. People who have their eyes wide open to what the world is really like. Who are willing to believe in the impossible. Someone just like you."

Thinking back to the odd tugging sensation that I'd experienced the night before, I frowned.

He spoke now in a lower whisper. "I know you can feel it."

"And?"

He leaned so far that he breached the center of the table. "You're here for a reason. We all are. Some come to expand the town through business and whatnot. Others to cause trouble."

"So you think I'm trouble?"

Atticus smiled. "I know you are."

He had a fair point there.

"And the people who are drawn here? What are they like?" I said.

"Nonhuman."

"Huh." I hadn't expected him to come right out and say it. Most creatures that I'd met on my travels liked to keep such things private.

"Let me get this straight. Because some mystical force supposedly called me here, you think I'm a freak?" The table hid my hands from sight so he couldn't see my nails digging into my palms.

Atticus offered me a kind smile. "Some might call us that."

"Well," I snorted. "I wouldn't put that particular detail on your town's tourism brochures any time soon." With that, I pushed up to my feet, not bothering to say my next words in a whisper. "The waffles were good. Shame the company was lacking."

"I didn't mean to offend you," he called as I started to walk away.

"Offend me?" I laughed and turned back. It was only when I noticed several pairs of eyes looking in our direction that I hurried back.

"You just implied that I'm a freak," I said in an angry whisper. "What's to be offended about?"

"Please." He motioned to my empty seat. "Let me explain. I'm not saying this as well as I should be."

"Is this how you pick up the girls in town? By insulting them?" I shot him a withering glare. "Sorry. I'm not that kind of girl."

He shook his head. "Look, I get it. You're not used to being around your kind in such large quantities. It can be a little disconcerting at first."

"There are no others of my kind," I bit back.

Realizing I'd spoken too loud, I shoved into my chair to glare at him. The last thing I needed was to make a scene where people would remember my face. What with the burns and all, I was pretty easy to spot.

Atticus nodded. "We all felt that way when we first came here. Havenwood Falls is a sanctuary for supernaturals, or supes for short. The outside world is a harsh place, but we can live in peace here. Shifters, mages, fae, and the like. We can be normal."

Normal. I couldn't remember the last time I felt like I was.

"Look around you. The truth is right under your nose. You just have to really look," he said.

Glancing around, I noticed people watching me. For the first time, I realized several of them were not human. A girl with a feline scent sniffed the air and turned away. One man sitting in the far corner piqued my interest. He was enormous, with an extensive growth of hair covering every part of his body not hidden by the trench coat he wore. A wide-brimmed hat sat low over his eyes.

"Is that a . . ." I trailed off, feeling silly for even thinking something so outrageous.

Atticus glanced over his shoulder. "His name is Sherman. And yeah, he's a Bigfoot. Or a yeti, I think he prefers. He's new to town. Here visiting a friend that hides out in the woods, I've heard. They aren't very social creatures, as you can imagine. I'd never actually met one before Sherman. Havenwood Falls draws in all sorts. Pretty cool, huh?"

My mouth gaped at the thought of how this town would react if a camera crew from some TV show rolled into town. Man, would they get a rude awakening!

"Yeah. Cool." I spotted no fewer than six humans sitting in the room. Not a single one paid Sherman any mind.

"It's a glamour," I whispered as I discovered the majority of the busy room was nonhuman. A pair of vampires sat in a recessed corner. They returned to their conversations over cups of blood rather than of plates of food.

"I've never seen so many species mingling together. They aren't fighting," I whispered. Then I shook myself and looked at Atticus. "And what about you?"

"What about me?" He smiled.

"I can't quite figure out which supernatural you are."

"Ah." He grinned. "I'm a man of mystery."

I snorted. "Well, don't you go thinking that I don't see what's happening here. You assume that since I'm one of you that you can pour me a big ole glass of Kool-Aid. Figure I'll be eager to sign up for the crazy train."

Atticus grinned and sat back. "I knew I'd like you. From the moment I heard you giving crap to Lloyd, I knew."

I rolled my eyes and sank back into the seat. This was too much. The idea that an entire town of supernaturals existed blew my mind. How had they managed to bring peace and order to so many species? Thinking back to his uncle's black sedan that morning with the mixture of creatures, it made sense now. The blending was a natural occurrence here.

"I'm not saying the town is perfect," he added in his hushed tone. "Some of the personalities can be a bit strong. And there are skirmishes sometimes that break out. No one is perfect. But that's why our registry is important. It helps keep people in check."

That didn't sound good. "Does everyone have to register?"

"Sure do. Humans live here as well, but they don't know about us. We either assume human form while in town or use a glamour to conceal our real identity. Sometimes a memory charm is used if things get out of hand, but for the most part, it works. Some of the humans have relatives who come to visit. Others show up and decide to stick around. For them, it's a matter of a little paperwork and a background check. But for those of us with extra abilities, the registration process is a little more in-depth."

Ideas began to spiral through my mind. If everyone had to register, that meant there had to be a record of my momma's killer.

"You want to tell me why seeing that registry means so much to you?"

I blinked and looked up to meet his piercing gaze. *Crap.* I must have let my excitement show.

"You're right. I am here for a reason. I'm looking for someone."

When he nodded, a bit of sandy blond hair fell over his eye, and he brushed it away. "I figured as much."

"Everything all right over here?" Our waitress returned, balancing a steaming pot of coffee on her tray. She directed the question toward Atticus.

"We're good," Atticus said. "You know I'm a sucker for your waffles, Harlow."

The girl's long hair was pulled back from her face, revealing stunning eyes, cheekbones worthy of envy, and flawless skin. Her smile was just a shade too wide when she spoke to Atticus, twirling her hair around her finger like a pro.

I decided right then that I hated her. Not because she was beautiful, or charming, or god knows a gazillion things different than me. It was because she did it all with perfect ease. I hated people that could breeze through situations that made me cringe.

"Why don't you grab our check and bring it to me?" Atticus flashed me a smile. "I'm treating our new guest to the finest Havenwood Falls has to offer."

Harlow cut her eyes toward me. She did a poor job hiding her look of annoyance, but Atticus didn't take notice.

"Sure thing." Her heels clicked on the wood floor as she walked away.

"I don't need charity. I can pay my own way," I snapped the instant she was gone.

When his eyebrow hiked high enough to dust the ends of his hair, I knew he saw straight through that lie. "It's the least I can do, since I blackmailed you into joining me."

"You seem pretty good at that," I grumbled. Harlow had gotten under my skin for no good reason.

Sunlight caught the white streaks in his hair when he nodded. "I've had a bit of practice."

"I bet you have."

A man like Atticus was sure to have more than a few admirers in town. Not that I cared. Not one little bit.

"Our waitress likes you."

"Who? Harlow? She's a nice girl." Atticus smirked. "And you're changing the subject."

"So are you," I shot back.

For a moment, I thought he was going to jump into a battle of wit and words, but instead, he fell silent, watching me. Why did everyone around this place have to keep sizing me up?

"Who is he?"

"Huh?" I was confused.

"Your mark. The guy you're hunting."

43

"How do you know he's a he?" I challenged.

"Is he a lover? A long-lost soul mate?" He tapped his chin. "No. You don't seem the type for that."

"You're batting zero on the whole not offending me thing," I said.

His tawny gaze glowed pure gold when he leaned forward. Maybe it was a play of the sunlight streaming in through the windows, but I'd have bet money it wasn't.

"No," he mused. "You're looking for someone you hate."

Well, that's a bit too close for comfort.

"You know, for a super-secret town, y'all sure pry into people's business too much."

He reached out to take my hand. I flinched, but didn't rip my hand away. "You do a good job of hiding it, but I can sense your pain. This man took something from you. Something you loved."

I looked away, afraid he might stare long enough to see the terrified little girl still trapped there. Sliding my hand out from under his, I clasped mine together in my lap to stop them from shaking.

"My business is my own. Take a hint and butt out." I stood, and this time I didn't look back.

CHAPTER 7

It wasn't until I reached the sidewalk out front that I remembered I drove both of us to breakfast. I wasn't about to hop in a car with a stranger. Apparently he didn't have the same qualms.

"Bugger!" I stomped my foot. "Way to ruin a perfectly good exit."

"It's a lot easier to storm off when you don't have a passenger." Atticus chuckled from behind me as I marched toward the Jeep, but his long stride overtook me. "You could have left me behind. Thanks for sticking around."

"Like I really had a choice." I groaned. "Taking a hint isn't one of your strong suits, is it?"

"Nope. Well, I mean it usually is, but I like you."

"Gee. Lucky me."

He sank into the passenger seat beside me. Nice homes of varying shapes, sizes, and landscaping passed by as I picked up speed. It didn't take long to realize I would have been lost without Atticus guiding me. Why did they have to make the houses look so similar?

As I turned back onto Main Street and headed toward the town center, I realized those waffles were starting to fight me. The school parking lot we passed on the way was packed with cars. I weaved through the traffic.

"Where did all these cars come from? It's not a school day."

"The festival, remember? We have something every month. You'll love this one. The town goes all out with their costumes."

"Costumes?" When I glanced at the busy sidewalk, I realized several people were dressed in old-world style dresses. One man even had breeches and stockings on. "Oh, that is too funny!"

"Hey, don't knock the style. If you stick around long enough, you might just buy a dress."

"Not likely," I snickered.

The sleepy little town square had become a bustling mecca of trade. I hated crowds, but what better place to do some reconnaissance than right there? Turning into one of the last spaces available behind a row of apartments, I threw the car into park and distracted Atticus while I disconnected the wires.

"Is that guy carrying a lance?" I asked.

"Sure. Later this afternoon they will have a mini jousting tournament. My brother Orlon and I won it last year."

"Of course you did." I slammed the Jeep door behind me. "Is that . . . turkey legs I smell?"

Atticus grinned. "It wouldn't be a Renaissance faire without turkey legs. Come on."

His excitement made me smile as he ushered me toward the square. We passed by a quaint art studio and Pyntz Butcher Shoppe. Both had closed signs for the festivities. I noticed Lloyd's No Parking signs lined with anal perfection around the square as we crossed the street.

"Wait!" Atticus called as I darted out into traffic. Horns blared, and a few people shot me their middle finger, but I made it to the other side unharmed.

"Well, that was fun," he said a second later.

"Are you kidding me right now?" I turned to see him grinning. "Why did you—no. Never mind. I don't care. Please don't feel the need to escort me around. I'm perfectly capable of seeing the sights on my own."

"Of course you are." He raised a hand to wave at a couple decked out in their Renaissance attire. The little girl with them looked precious with ribbons tied into her hair. "But what's the fun in that?"

As we passed by a Tacos for Daze truck parked out front of the Haven Saloon, I winced and held my breath. There was no way I could eat another bite. A long line outside Coffee Haven told me that I'd been right about the clientele and how popular it would be.

"You weren't kidding about the crowds." I whistled as we joined a herd moving toward the park. Last night I'd slept to the peaceful sounds of the water fountain. Today, all I could hear was laughter and music in the air. I realized it was coming from speakers set up around the area.

"Wait until tonight. That's when the real fun starts."

Tonight? Well, it was official. I was stuck with Atticus. That much was clear. What wasn't clear was why. I was a nobody. A total stranger who had established I had a chip on my shoulder. Yet Atticus stayed glued to my side. He pointed out some of the vendors, rattling off details about who they were and what businesses they ran, most of which I refused to admit were actually interesting.

He introduced me to Rhys Graywalk, the owner of the Dirty Knuckle, who was passing out a few samples of libations despite the fact that five o'clock was a long way off. Atticus offered me a frothy beer in a plastic cup, but I turned him down. No sense revealing that I was still underage.

Next, we came to a booth ran by Rhiannon Underwood, gardener extraordinaire from Fairy Tale Florists. Even though flowers weren't my thing, hearing Rhiannon talk about the predatory aspects of a Venus fly trap to a little girl was pretty cool. She'd just started giving a presentation about plants used to make deadly concoctions in the dark ages when Atticus dragged me on.

Charlotte Ramsay ran a booth for Shear Magic, situated just out front of her shop. Atticus got a good laugh when Charlotte offered me a discount on a waxing. Bastard.

Havenwood Falls Medical Center had a booth set up, but I steered clear of that. No sense tempting fate. But the staff did look hilarious in their jester costumes.

"What about this one?" Atticus asked.

"Oh, heck no." I practically ran from the Tragic Ink booth.

"Got something against tattoos?" Atticus didn't even try to hide his smile.

"That's none of your business," I huffed, annoyed that I'd let him see my weakness. I didn't care how childish it was. Needles were evil!

As the hours went by, it was easy to see how ingrained Atticus was in the town. He knew everyone, and they certainly knew him. His easygoing manner was popular with the buxom ladies. He was the target of a couple obvious advances, but he was a gentleman in his rejections.

I found myself watching him as we wandered through the crowds. He stood a head taller than most, and his broad frame cleared a path for me.

"It's ok to stare," he said over his shoulder as we passed the turkey drumstick food truck that smelled like heaven on wheels. I was pretty sure I smelled funnel cake too.

"At what?" I asked.

"My butt. I know you want to."

That sent me into a fit of giggles. I couldn't remember the last time I laughed like that.

"There it is." He wagged a finger at me. "I knew it was there, hidden under that sexy little scowl of yours."

I stopped walking. "Sexy?"

"Well, yeah." He scratched at the thin layer of beard growth. "You have looked in the mirror, right?"

More times than I cared to admit. I knew what was there, and it was nothing special.

"Hey," he whispered and gently took hold of my chin. "I know that look. I've seen it before."

He brushed my hair back from my face and let his gaze fall over my scars. "Why must it always be the good ones who never see their true beauty?"

I wanted to scoff and crack a joke about his lame pickup line, but somehow I knew it wasn't one. His smile was too genuine and his eyes sincere. It made me wonder who in his life had taught him such compassion.

"Well." I blew out a breath. "You just made this awkward."

"I did, didn't I?" He laughed and let his hand drop away. But when I caught him watching me, I couldn't help but smile. He had that way about him.

We made the rounds of the festival vendors three times before I allowed myself to admit defeat. My momma's killer wasn't here. But it sure seemed like everyone else in town was.

I allowed myself to be dragged to a play set up on a small stage placed in the gazebo. It would have been mind-numbingly boring if not for the fact that one of the bumbling characters reminded me of Lloyd. I hid my smile until Atticus bumped my arm.

"I saw that."

"Did not." But I didn't mind that he'd seen. The day had turned out to actually be nice. Far better than what I'd expected.

As the crowds dispersed, many people rushing to line up for the food trucks again, I sank down onto a bench to people-watch. Atticus sat with me, content to be silent for a while.

"So what's the deal with tonight?"

He glanced at me. "What?"

"You said that there was more." And more might mean a sighting of my momma's killer.

"Oh." He nodded his head at an older woman. I think he'd told me she was Mabel, who worked at Broastful Brew. Somehow the kind woman, and her less trendy coffee shop, seemed more Atticus's style. And mine, for that matter. "The daytime activities are for everyone. The ones that happen tonight, well . . . let's just say it's a bit of a free-for-all."

My eyebrow hiked. "Meaning?"

He leaned in close. His arm, slung over the back of the bench, brushed along my back as he whispered in my ear, "You ever see that movie *The Purge*?"

I snorted. "You're kidding."

"Nope." He moved back but didn't remove his arm. "Now I'm not going to say that it's that bad, but things can get pretty wild around here."

"Wild?" I laughed. That seemed hardly the sort of thing that would happen in a place like this, but then again, I now understood what lived here. "You going?"

This time, Atticus hesitated. "Maybe."

I shifted to look at him. "You scared?"

He laughed and shook his head. "No. I can handle myself. It's just . . . it's not my thing."

I watched him for a moment, trying to decipher his meaning. "It bothers you, doesn't it?"

Atticus kept his gaze focused on a shop called Room across the street. It was located just behind Broastful Brew and had a dove-gray awning. The front was a clean white brick with two lovely trees planted in wooden boxes. There was nothing noteworthy about the building that would require his candid study. That's when I noticed that he was watching a woman pacing in the window.

"Someone special?" I asked.

He blinked and then looked at me. "Who? Melissa? Nah. She's just been through a lot recently. My aunt loves fine art, and Room has the best in town. Melissa's son Harry is—was—a godsend." Atticus's expression grew somber as he clasped his hands in his lap. "I can't imagine how hard it must have been on Melissa to lose him. Especially knowing her new baby was due not long after."

"You know, I don't know many guys who would care about someone that much." And that was the darn truth. "You've got this knack for putting other people, even strangers, first, don't you?"

He smiled. "Trust me, some days it's a curse."

"Maybe." I offered him a small smile back. "But the world needs more men like you."

"Is that a compliment I hear?"

I laughed and shrugged. "Maybe."

He leaned back into the bench, folded his hands over his chest and grinned. "I'll take it."

A man entered the shop, and I heard the small tinkle of a bell over the door. I watched as Melissa moved to greet her customer. Room was one of the few shops that hadn't chosen to have a vendor table for the fair, but I supposed she wouldn't want to risk damaging her son's art.

She looked to be around forty, with long legs, perfectly blond hair and a tiny waist that made me feel even more insecure.

"I bet yoga is her miracle cure for post-pregnancy weight," I muttered and instantly felt a stab of guilt. Hadn't Atticus just told me that this woman had experienced a great deal of pain recently? *I am a terrible person.*

"Want a snow cone?" Atticus said, breaking into my thoughts.

"You've got a thing for food, don't you?"

He shrugged. "There's a high probability that I have a sweet tooth. Besides, it's sticky hot."

He was right about that. The humidity levels had risen since that morning. One glance at the clouds told me that there was a storm brewing. "I'm good."

"You sure? I'm buying."

"Go," I laughed.

"Fine. Your loss." He moved to stand in a long line outside a colorful stand.

The scent of sugar and ripe fruit was heavy in the air. Closing my eyes, I breathed it all in. If this had been a real Renaissance faire, there might have been animal feces lining small paddocks. Thankfully, this town went with the more sanitary bunnies in cages and a few chickens for sale.

That's when I caught the sound of a voice I recognized. My eyes popped open, and I searched the crowd.

It was him.

Standing at a booth on the other side of the street, I saw my momma's killer stooped low in conversation.

"Got you." I darted through the crowd, wishing I was as big as Atticus as I tried to push my way through. Several people cried out when I shoved them aside. A little girl burst into tears when I hit her from behind and she lost her grip on a red balloon. Guilt wiggled through me as I watched it rise into the sky.

"Sorry!" But my apology meant nothing to that little girl. I wanted to stop, to go back and offer to buy her a new one, but I didn't have time. The man was already walking away, heading toward the long line of cars that weaved down the street.

"Stop!" I yelled.

Though several people around me paused to watch as I rushed past, my momma's killer did not.

"Get out of my way!" I leaped over a booth that had been set on its end to tear down for the evening. The tablecloth flapped in the wind and caught my foot. I hit the ground hard, knocking the wind out of me.

"Are you okay?"

I groaned and looked up into Atticus's face. "Why do you always show up during the embarrassing moments?"

"Well, you do have quite a few of them." When he helped me to a seated position, I fought to see around his shoulders, but it was too late. The man was gone.

"No!" I beat my fist into the ground.

Atticus's eyes narrowed. "Care to tell me what that was all about? You tore this place apart like it was nothing."

I shoved my hair back out of my face and glared. "I saw him. Thanks to you and those people in my way, I lost him."

"Whoa." He held up his hands. "I don't seem to remember standing in your way when you took off like a bat out of hell."

"Not then." I rubbed the raw skin on my elbows. "Earlier. You were distracting me."

Atticus's mouth opened and closed. When he chuckled, I rolled my eyes. "Oh, don't let that go to your head. I meant you were talking too much, made me lose my focus. Not that you're hot or anything."

"So you have noticed then?" That perfect grin was back.

"Is everything okay over here? That girl took quite a fall," Mabel asked, giving me an out. I hadn't managed to run very far at all—I was still in front of Broastful Brew. *Well, that was pathetic.* Not to mention embarrassing. I glanced up to see Melissa looking out at me from the window of her shop.

"She's fine. Her hard head broke the fall." Atticus helped me to my feet and used his body to shield me from sight. "It might help if I had something to call you when I'm chasing you. 'Hey you' doesn't seem to work too well."

"Ember," I muttered, still wallowing in frustration and no small amount of embarrassment. I really had made a scene.

"Ember? That's hot."

I glanced back at him and saw that his familiar lopsided grin was fixed in place. "Congratulations, you tricked me into telling you."

He tugged on the collar of his flannel shirt. With a puffed-up chest, he did a little strut that made me laugh. "Stick around long enough, Ember, and you'll realize I've got skills."

I glanced past him to the tearful little girl and sighed. "If you really want to help, take this and get that girl a new balloon."

He stared at the crumpled dollars I'd placed in his palm. "Well, aren't you a softy."

I snorted. "Hardly."

A light rain began to fall as I waited for Atticus to buy a new balloon. I didn't notice it at first. But as the sky began to darken and the winds increased, rolling off the mountains, I knew we were in fact in for a good storm. All around us, people rushed to cover their tables.

"Hey," he said when he hurried back over. "I'm sorry you lost your guy. It's a small town. We'll find him again. But I'd advise against doing it tonight."

"Right. The whole Purge thing. But wouldn't that be the best time?"

"Nope." He steered me back toward my car. "Trust me. You don't want to be anywhere near town for that. We'll find him tomorrow."

"I've been hunting him for six years. He's not an easy man to catch."

"Six years?" He whistled. "He must have hurt you pretty bad."

Droplets of rain pattered my face as the heavens opened. Atticus took my hand and led me through the chaos of vendors tearing down. Before my foot could land on the sidewalk, Atticus pushed me against the side of a food truck. He stepped in front of me to block my view.

"What are you doing? It's pouring!" I said.

"Look."

I stopped grumbling at him when I saw a boot clamp on the front tire of my Jeep. Lloyd was no longer alone. Several other cops wearing rain ponchos now surrounded the vehicle. The driver's side door was open, and one officer was poking around, searching under the seat.

Atticus glanced at me, but I said nothing.

"Here." He pressed a set of keys into my hand and pointed down the street. "Take mine. It's that black Subaru two blocks down. Ignore the cloud of smoke that'll follow you. The muffler is junk."

I opened my fingers to see a car key surrounded by several others. "You're loaning me your car?"

He nodded. "The gold key is for my cabin. It's not much. Just a small place up Miles Mountain. Take the main road back out of town. Take the first right after the town sign. You'll find the cabin about three miles up on the right. It's an A-frame set out on a rocky ridge."

"Why are you doing this?" I stared at him, trying to commit his directions to memory. "You don't owe me anything."

Atticus nodded. "I already told you. I'm a nice guy. Besides, I'd rather know you make it to morning. Sticking around town isn't a good idea. Especially for someone like you."

CHAPTER 8

Waking up in a strange place had a way of messing with my mind. Especially when the waking came as a pounding on the cabin door that rattled my brain. Oh, and then there was the fact that I had to maneuver a rickety ladder as my only escape from the sleeping loft.

My foot slipped, and I dropped a couple of rungs before I caught myself. Pain flared when my chin smacked into the wood.

"Son of a—" I gritted my teeth.

From the other side of the door, there came a throaty laugh, and I groaned. I should've known it would be Atticus. I was shacked up in his home after all.

The door creaked as I opened it. "I'd tell you to go away, but I know you won't."

"Of course not."

He gave me an appraising glance as I rubbed my chin. I'd been soaked by the time I arrived. With my spare set of clothes trapped in the backseat of the stolen Jeep, I'd had no choice but to go digging through his drawers. I'd found a faded Led Zeppelin shirt and claimed it. But now, standing in front of him wearing only that, I realized how little it covered.

"That shirt looks way better on you than it does me." He winked and pushed past me into the room. He'd definitely noticed that it barely covered my backside.

He kicked the door closed with his foot, while somehow managing not to spill a single drop of coffee. His display of coordination skills at this time of the morning royally ticked me off.

"I brought coffee and doughnuts," he said with an upbeat tone.

Of course, he's a morning person.

I slumped into one of the two wooden chairs and buried my head in my hands. Atticus bustled around the small kitchen. The clatter of metal plates made my head hurt. I squinted at the cups of coffee in front of me and lunged, knocking the table back a few inches.

"Whoa!" Atticus slid into the seat across from me and braced the table. "Heaven help the person who comes between you and your caffeine."

I glared at him, but his smile never faltered. He really seemed to enjoy taunting me.

"Sleep well?" he asked.

Taking a long, scalding sip of my liquid mojo, I shrugged. "The bed is lumpy."

"Huh." He frowned and glanced at the loft. "I never noticed."

Setting aside my cup, I sighed. Thanking people wasn't something I was good at.

"Thanks for not asking questions yesterday and for lending me your car so I could crash here. And I guess for breakfast, again."

"Wow." Atticus chuckled and shook his head. "That must have hurt to say."

"You have no idea." I scowled and gripped my cup tighter.

He grinned, seeming quite pleased with my reaction. Then he made a show of plating up our gourmet breakfast of sprinkle donuts and bear claws. The funny thing was that they actually did resemble a real claw.

"Did you buy me pink on purpose?" I glared at the offensive color. I hated when guys assumed that because I had different anatomy, I was fond of pink.

"What? Oh." He reached over and shoved a chocolate donut in my direction instead. "Sorry. That one is for me."

It was a good thing I wasn't trying to drink at that moment, because I spit all over myself. Although I hadn't known him long, I'd come to realize that I didn't have one stinkin' clue how his mind worked.

"What?" he said with a giant mouthful of glazed dough. "I'm man enough to admit that I like a little pink in my life."

As I watched, he downed the whole pastry in two bites. Now that was impressive. I took longer with mine. Although sugar and I were good friends, my stomach had no desire to wake up this early.

I looked around the cabin as the sky began to lighten. Wooden planks lined the walls, some straighter than others. The floors were roughly hewn. A sliding glass door to my right looked out over the valley. Puffy spray can insulation peeked through the cracks around the unfinished door. No curtains or blinds hung to conceal the view of the town below.

Next to the door was a small kitchen with the bare essentials. A rack hung from the ceiling, stocked with a couple cast iron pots and pans. The remaining camp plates and mugs stood on a handmade shelf. The small countertop led my gaze to a cozy seating area with a well-used couch and a wood burning stove.

The kitchen table we sat at filled the center of the space. A ladder led up to the sleeping loft. It held one bed, a nightstand, and a lantern that I hadn't bothered to light the night before. I'd been so exhausted by the time I arrived at his cabin that I'd only taken time to check the perimeter. Then I barricaded the doors, stripped out of my wet clothes and passed out. I wondered where Atticus had spent the night.

"You built this place, didn't you?" I asked, fiddling with the hem of his T-shirt that I wore. It smelled of him, like everything else in this place.

"Sure did." Atticus wiped frosting from his lips.

His day's growth looked good on him this morning. I was glad that I'd bunked in his house long enough to prevent him from shaving. There was something so irresistibly sexy about a man with a bit of scruff.

"It took me most of the fall and winter to get the frame up. That's a slow time for me at work, so I had more time to spare. There are a few things that still need doing. I don't have electricity or any running water, either, so you'll have to forgo a shower. But I can haul up some water if you'd like a bath."

"I'm good," I hurried to say. The idea of him being close at such an intimate time stained my cheeks with a blush.

"The outhouse is back by the tree line," he continued. "I know that's not what you're used to—"

"Fine by me," I cut him off. "I just used a tree."

I wasn't some soft city girl who needed luxuries. I'd slept in my fair share of bus stops, public restroom stalls, and a few abandoned subway cars. I knew how to make do, and for some reason, it mattered to me that he understood that.

"Well, I guess that's the tour then. You can stay as long as you need to." I shot a quick glance up at the sleeping loft with its compact bed and then looked away again. "I'll take the couch. No sense making this awkward."

When he stretched his arms over his head, the bottom of his flannel shirt parted enough to reveal a tease of muscle. I smirked and looked away, knowing that he'd given me that eyeful on purpose.

"I know this is your place and all, but why exactly are you here?" I asked, pushing away the remaining crumbs of breakfast. I'd lost what little appetite I'd had.

"Oh." He grabbed my plate and spun toward the sink. It was only a few feet away, so it wasn't quite as an impressive feat as his coffee balancing act earlier. "It's Sunday, so I've got the whole day off for a bit of sleuthing."

I groaned. I knew he was going to say that.

"Now, don't you go griping at me." He shook a small scrub brush in my direction. I realized with a great amount of surprise that he was actually doing dishes.

Wow. This guy was the whole package.

"You need help, and I'm the man for the job."

"And if I say no?"

He shot me that sexy lopsided grin of his, and I knew it'd become my kryptonite. "You aren't the only stubborn one in town. Besides, I know people. Good people with tracking skills."

When he turned back to cleaning our two plates, I tapped my fingers against the coffee cup. Maybe it wasn't a terrible idea. He knew everyone. And he did want to help.

"Are you on friendly terms with any demons?" I asked.

Atticus went still. "No."

"Sure about that?"

He glanced over his shoulder at me. "Few people are. At least not the kind of people you want to hang out with."

I nodded. That was true enough. I'd heard rumors there were some demons that were actually halfway decent. They were a hybrid of sorts that somehow enabled them to maintain a sliver of their soul. That was hard for me to wrap my mind around. A demon was bad, no matter how you looked at it. And by bad, I meant BAD. I usually avoided them at all costs.

When I looked up, he was watching me. "You think this guy you're after is a demon?"

"To be honest, I'm not sure what he is. I haven't been able to pin anything solid on him, and believe me, I've tried."

Atticus sank back into his seat, drying his hands on a small rag. "So what do you know?"

"He killed my momma on my birthday."

He closed his eyes and shook his head. "I'm sorry, Ember. If I'd known—"

"It's fine." I looked away, feeling the familiar tightening in my throat. Even after all this time, it was still hard to talk about it. "It wasn't a good death. She burned alive in front of me. At night, I can still hear her screams when I'm drifting off to sleep."

I paused, needing a moment to get my emotions in check. "Southern gentlemen and proper belles surrounded me as a child in Savannah. My momma raised me to be a lady, to make her daddy proud, I'm sure. I'd attended the finest schools and trained with the best ballet company in Georgia. Dancing has given me an edge when fighting these days, but I'd never admit to it."

Atticus grinned at that.

"High society taught me that people could be kind to their own when they chose to be. Which was mighty fine until my thirteenth birthday. That's the night my momma died and I became an orphan. Then I learned how cold and unfeeling my momma's 'friends' could be."

"I'm sorry." And I knew he meant it.

"That was also the night I entered this new world. One where monsters hid in the shadows, waiting to take me out. A girl learned a thing or two mighty quick when she had to." I paused. I didn't think I'd ever told anyone this story before. "My momma's death left my emotions a bit unstable. Several other fires occurred over the months that followed. I guess my granddaddy figured I was the reason his little girl was gone. He blamed me, disowned me, and turned me over to the state. I never saw him or his money again. Disreputable foster care families were the least of my worries after that."

His eyes grew wide. "And this demon started the fire?"

"I've asked myself that same question more times than I can count. No matter how hard I try to remember, I just can't."

Back then, I hadn't been aware of my abilities or that supernaturals were even a real thing. After that, I spent days digging into lore. I was desperate to piece together the shards of memory that I had from that night. When I'd learned that a traumatic event could release dormant powers, I'd begun to suspect that I was to blame.

"What little family I had left after Momma died didn't want to deal with my oddities. I bounced from home to home after that. None of them fit well. I seemed to cause trouble everywhere I went, so after a while, I stopped caring. Then I found a few people who were different, like me. Some were kind and taught me the way of things. Others put a dagger in my hand and tossed me into a fighting ring. I learned real quick how to defend myself."

Atticus's mouth fell open. "They forced you to fight? That's barbaric."

"I didn't have a Havenwood Falls to grow up in. The real world isn't like this place." I shrugged. "My first fight was when I was fourteen. I'd been placed in a foster home with an angel."

His brow creased with lines of confusion. "Wouldn't that be a good thing?"

"They aren't all cute little harps and rainbows, Atticus." A bitter laugh rumbled in my chest as I scooted to the side on my chair. He glanced over as I lifted the T-shirt to reveal a ten-inch scar that ran up my thigh. "That Seraph blade nearly took my leg clean off. Cut clear to the bone faster than I could react. I got a few good swipes in on my own. It took almost a full week of intense healing before I could walk again. Needless to say, when I skipped out of the hospital, I decided that home wasn't for me."

Atticus didn't react to the speed with which I'd managed to recover from such a severe wound. That betrayed that he knew all about healing powers. I wondered if he possessed them himself or had seen them in action.

He remained silent with his hands clenched into tight fists on the table. The muscle in his jaw clenched as he ground his teeth. The depth of his concern touched me, but I reminded myself I didn't care.

"The next place, a small town in Florida's panhandle, ran me smack dab into a witch's coven. I stuck around there for a while. They took a liking to me. After a while, I moved on. I knew I wasn't going to find my momma's killer there, and having them take care of me was making me soft."

I looked toward the glass window. The mists had finally begun to burn off, and the sun shone brightly, but it did nothing to lift my mood.

"I traveled around the Deep South for several years. When the cops would catch up with me, I'd find myself bounced into a new home. School had its uses, but I never stuck around long enough to make friends." I fell silent for a moment. Some of the things that'd happened to me weren't relevant, so I kept those to myself. "New Orleans was a scary place. Why tourists think voodoo is cute is beyond me. I saw things there that will haunt me until I die, but that's where I found my first clue two years ago."

"How'd you end up here?" The chair creaked as he leaned back on two legs.

Rubbing at the scar on my hip, I laid out the details of how I'd come to live with Susan after my brief stint in New Orleans. Of hearing rumors about other children going missing. Most of those cases turned out to be the results of sick-minded humans with a thing for kids. Then I'd stumbled across a troll in Albuquerque who'd told me about a snitch for a fair price: my momma's gold watch. It broke my heart to hand it over, but I knew it'd be worth it if the information rang true.

I amended the finer details about my fight with Fluffy, choosing to leave out the parts where he was a three-headed wolf and that he'd put me in the hospital. Some things were best not known. That included the details about my abilities.

After I skipped the gruesome parts, I caught him up to when I ran him over with the Jeep. He laughed when he realized that Lloyd had actually gotten something right. "So you really did steal that car?"

"Of course I did. Do I look like a Jeep kind of girl to you?"

He gave me a long look that made a warm blush rise to my cheeks. "Nah. But I could see you on a bike."

Now that was an idea I could get on board with. I'd always had a thing for black and leather. Adding a motorcycle on top seemed like a good next step.

When his hand fell over mine, I flinched and jerked my gaze up to meet his. "I'm sorry that your life has been so hard. I can't even imagine what it must have been like. I promise I'll help you find the scumbag who killed your mom."

For the first time, I was at a loss for words.

"But first," he shoved up to his feet and held out his hand to me, "we need to get you registered."

CHAPTER 9

*R*egistration wasn't as bad as I thought it would be. The paperwork went fast enough once I figured out a new false identity to roll with. I'd used many over the years, but a few of those covers were blown. Atticus told me the fake name wouldn't work, but what did he know about lying low from the law? He was Mr. Perfect.

While I waited for the test results to confirm that I wasn't human, I wondered if it could tell me my species. The thought both excited and unnerved me. I'd gone so long without knowing that the idea of finally discovering the truth made me almost nauseous.

"What's got your panties in a twist?" Atticus asked from behind a magazine. He flipped the page, but didn't look at me.

"Who says they are?" I countered.

"Your knee is bouncing ninety miles an hour. FYI, that jangling your boots are doing is making it hard to focus on this fascinating article."

I looked over at him and smirked. Yanking the magazine out of his hands, I turned it over. "It helps if you hold it the right way up when you're pretending not to check me out."

He didn't look the least bit embarrassed. We both knew he'd been eyeing me up all day. I guess seeing me scantily clad in his Led Zeppelin T-shirt had made quite an impression on him. I wished that I could say his flannel shirt was a total turnoff. I usually wasn't into that whole lumberjack thing, but he made it look good.

In need of a serious derailment from those thoughts, I focused on my surroundings instead. A nondescript maintenance door had led us to the registry office. It was a good cover-up. I hadn't expected this part of City Hall to look so normal. A few swords on the walls, maybe a steaming caldron or toads in jars would have felt more realistic than this waiting room.

"You're doing it again." He set aside the magazine and forced me to drag my thoughts back to him. When he placed a hand on my knee to stop the bouncing, I had to force myself not to swat him away. That would be childish. Not to mention it would have given me another reason to touch him.

"How much information does that blood work give?" I asked, pushing aside the thoughts of where else I'd like to touch him.

He watched me for a moment. "Afraid your blood is going to rat you out? I told you that fake name wouldn't help. Blood doesn't lie, especially when Addie is back there, working her magic."

I sighed and slumped into my chair. His statement wasn't a figure of speech. I'd smelled magic in the room the moment I walked in. "The opposite, actually."

"Wait a second." Atticus leaned toward me.

"You really don't know what you are, do you?"

My scowl was already firmly in place before he finished his sentence. "I told you that I'm the only one."

He shook his head. "No way. There's always more than one."

"Yeah?" I poked him in the chest. The muscle was firm and way too tempting, so I pulled back. "Well, I've been a lot of places, and I've never met anyone like me."

"So what can you do? Shift? Fly? Talk to the dead?" Atticus turned toward me in his seat. "Wait! Are you already dead? I'm not into that sort of thing, but I could make an exception for you."

He sniffed the air like he'd be able to smell the rot right off me. I smacked him on the arm, making sure to connect with bare skin for the added sting effect.

"What was that for?"

"For sniffing me without asking."

"Fair enough." He laughed and waved an invisible flag of surrender. "But you still haven't given me any hints."

"Huh." I looked away from him and stared at the cat poster on the far wall. Cats creeped me out. Especially the cute cuddly ones. Somehow the girl who worked here didn't seem the sort to like stupid cats either. I'd bet money that someone stuck it up there as a joke. "I wonder why that is."

"Oh, come on, Ember." He nudged me with his shoulder. "I'll show you mine if you show me yours."

From the corner of my eye, I saw him wiggle his eyebrows suggestively, and a small laugh escaped me.

"Ember Ramsey?"

My head shot up at the announcement of my real name. Atticus muttered a "told you so" under his breath as I stood and walked through the door. I followed behind a girl a few years older than me. In her mid-twenties, she knew how to rock wide leather bracelets. With her ripped-up jeans and a diamond nose ring, I knew she was my kind of girl.

"How you doing, Addie? Haven't seen you in a while. Is the Court keeping you locked up?" Atticus asked as we entered what appeared to be a large courtroom and headed toward a desk in the back corner.

"Oh, I'm still around." Addie grinned and moved toward the far wall. "It's you that's a no-show these days. How's the landscaping business keeping you, now that summer is here?"

"Busy as always. You know Orlon, always cracking the whip. I'm lucky to get a day off."

A twinge of guilt hit me. Atticus had made it seem like it was no big deal to spend yesterday and today with me. Was he skipping out on work for me?

Addie turned to look back at him. "How is your brother doing? I saw Orlon yesterday, but he kept to himself. He downed his fair share of beers over at the Dirty Knuckle last night. When I went over to say hi, he grunted and stumbled away."

Atticus's shoulders took on a distinct slump. "Thanks for keeping an eye on him. It's been tough, but he'll find a way to move on when he's ready."

Addie smiled and reached out to squeeze his hand. "It's been tough for you, too. If you ever need to talk, you know where to find me."

"Thanks."

A tingling in my palms flared to life in response to Addie's friendly offer, and I closed my fists.

Did I almost fry that girl because she was nice to Atticus?

No. She'd touched him and made it seem so effortless. Like they'd done it countless times before.

Jealous much?

A puff of smoke burst from my palm. I coughed and waved my hand to conceal the evidence.

"Sorry. Is it a bit warm in here to you guys?" It was a totally lame way to disperse the smoke, but it worked when they both shrugged and shook their heads.

I winced when they turned away. I was turning into one of those girls. Ugh.

The more time I spent with Atticus, the more I began to realize that he wasn't like other guys. There was something between us. I wasn't into that love at first sight crap. I'd stopped believing in fairy tales a long time ago. But I knew chemistry when I smelled it, and we had a lot of it.

Addie motioned for me to sit in a chair beside a desk. "Sit there. I'll just be a minute."

As soon as my eyes fell on her tattooing tools, I was done. There were few things that made me nervous in this world. Creepy dentists and tattoo artists were among them. Another glance at her tray of tools and ink told me that I was in the wrong place.

"Oh, heck no!" I was out of that chair and trying to push past Atticus in a heartbeat. "You never said anything about getting a tattoo."

Addie snickered at me as Atticus rolled his eyes. "This again? Are you telling me that the girl who took down an angel can't stand a little needle?"

"Whoa." There was a splash of liquid behind me as Addie whipped around. "You took on an angel? What was that like?"

I glared at the girl. "It wasn't a full takedown. More like a mutual truce after we got pretty bloody. I managed to land a few good blows."

"Wicked." She grinned and handed me a cup. "Drink this."

I sniffed it first. "What is it?"

"It's water. You look like you could use something a bit stiffer, but it's the best I've got."

Atticus gave me a quick nod, so I knocked it back. The liquid was about as tasteless as water, but it had a silky texture to it. A soothing sensation started to come over me. My grip on Atticus's hands loosened. The hammering of my heart slowed, and my gaze sank to the floor.

"Hey! I like your boots. I always thought combats were the best," I said with a slurred voice. Atticus smiled at me as he led me back to the chair. "What's wrong with my words? Did you drug me?"

"Of course not." But by the way he said it, I knew I'd been suckered.

"That's not cool." I glared at each of them in turn, but only innocent faces looked back at me. Four of them, actually. This stuff worked fast.

When a set of straps latched over my wrists, I realized that Atticus had tied me to the chair. "What are you doing?"

"The calming tincture is only temporary," Addie spoke with a soft tone. She moved toward the wall, and the lights dimmed around me. "Sometimes it's best to make sure you can't go anywhere, in case you try to bolt before I'm done. It's for your own safety."

I pressed my head back into the headrest, vowing that if this hurt as much as I thought it would, I was going to burn them. Nothing major. Enough to leave a mark. The trouble was I wasn't sure which one of them to hit first.

The sound of the tattoo pen humming to life made me dig my nails into the armrests. I hated that sound.

"All right, Ember." Addie's face appeared in front of me. "What would you like?"

"For you to get the heck away from me." My lips had started to go numb, and my head was definitely heavier than normal.

She grinned and tapped her chin. "Something fierce and deadly like you."

Atticus's head bobbed in agreement. "Got any good ideas?"

Addie's instant grin worried me. "I've got just the thing for you. Don't sweat it."

But I did. A lot. Sweat dripped into my eyes. It collected in the scooped neck of my tank as the pen pressed against my skin. Addie was much stronger than she looked. One hand clamped hard on my wrist while Atticus stroked my free hand. He acted like he would've liked to hold that hand, but I kept it gripped to the seat.

"It will all be over soon. I promise." His touch might have been soothing if I wasn't left wishing I could singe his pants for putting me here in the first place.

"All done." Addie sat back and placed the silent pen to the side.

"What? Already?" I blinked. My vision was a little fuzzy as I looked around. Atticus had somehow switched sides to stand with Addie. "How did you—"

"Why did you choose that design?" Atticus cut through my question.

"I don't know." Addie's shoulders rose and fell with a shrug. "It just came to me. You know, sometimes I get these feelings."

The two shared a long look at my tattoo before they turned toward me. As she unbuckled the strap around my left wrist, fear rose up in me. Fear that I couldn't quite contain under their sharp gaze.

"Go on then." Addie smiled, but it didn't look quite so confident now. "Tell me what you think."

Lifting my arm, I stared at the colorful new addition to my body. A beautiful firebird now took up half of my inner forearm. Its wings were the color of my hair, tipped in gold and vibrant oranges. Shock stole my breath away when the tattoo suddenly opened its wings wide.

"It moved!"

"What?" Addie reached for my hand, but Atticus beat her to it.

He yanked on my arm, and together we watched the bird ruffle its feathers. It turned its head, the brilliant fiery plume fluttering as if touched by the wind. Then its feathers began to shimmer. The gold became blinding, and I had to look away.

Atticus yanked Addie to her feet. "What the heck did you do to her?"

Her brow creased in confusion. "I don't see anything."

"What do you mean you don't see anything?" The planes of Atticus's face went rigid. "That tattoo burst into flames."

I rubbed my finger across the tattoo. He was right. That's exactly what the bird had done. But before that, it had shimmered with the same glittering color of my healing tears.

My breath caught. I recognized this creature from my search into lore. "This is a phoenix, isn't it?"

Addie and Atticus both turned to look at me. Addie nodded. "It is. The first I've ever done."

Atticus's face was pale. His hands shook where he still held Addie.

"Does it mean anything?" I whispered.

"No." Atticus said at the exact moment Addie said, "Yes."

He glared at her and then seemed to come to his senses. He released his grip on her arm and backed away. Small red markings where his fingers had been were highlighted against her pale skin.

I stared long and hard at him, but he refused to meet my gaze.

"I'll be outside." With that, he turned and hurried out of the room.

"What was that all about?" I asked.

Addie stared for a good minute in silence at the door. "He's still trying to get used to magic. Even for those raised knowing about the supernatural, it's sometimes hard to accept."

"And my tattoo? You didn't see it move?"

Worry creased the corner of her eyes. "I wasn't meant to see it."

"Meaning what?" I unbuckled my other hand and slid out of the seat.

I watched as she tugged at the sleeve of her hoodie. It was a bit frayed there, evidence that she liked to worry in that spot. "Infusing magic into our tattoos to uphold the town's warding isn't a science, Ember. Sometimes things just happen. Things that even I can't understand. Like the vision I had of your phoenix."

I looked at the bird. It seemed to be as agitated as I felt.

"You said a moment ago that my tattoo means something."

"Usually people tell me what they want. Like a clan emblem or something. But then other times I have to get a sense of a person from their blood to determine what fits best. Magic is about intent, Ember. I have to infuse the right kind of magic into the ink, and that requires working with the facts. With you, I saw fire." She looked a bit flustered when I stared back at her. I bet I looked as confused as I felt. "You do know why that is, right?"

"No."

She rubbed the back of her head and thought for a moment. It looked like she was working to choose her words. I wished she would just spit it out already. "With each tattoo that I give comes a magical benefit based on your species—"

"And what is my cool new gift?" I interrupted.

"For vampires, it allows them to be out in daylight. For you, it will be something different. Something that can help guide you with your own personal abilities."

"Great." That's when I realized she knew. She had to know. What with all of her talk about intentional magic and blood work. Addie knew full well what my species was, and for some reason, she wasn't sharing. "What am I?"

Her image swirled as a few rebellious tears snuck through, but not before I caught her hard glance. "You really don't know, do you?"

I shook my head. "There was no one left to tell me."

Addie sighed and placed her hand over my tattoo. "The truth is inside you, Ember. Sometimes people know deep down what they are, but they aren't ready to hear it. My guess is that you're scared. You want to know the truth but are too afraid to admit it. It's just like how you must sense why only you and Atticus saw your tattoo move."

"I don't. Sense anything, I mean." I wiped at my nose with a spare tissue she handed me.

Addie sighed again. I was pretty sure right about then she was ready to give me a good knock on the head to get me thinking straight. I would have welcomed that if I thought it would help. "Have you ever stopped to wonder if maybe all of the facts you need are right in front of you?"

I blinked. "I think I would have figured it out by now if that were true."

"One would think." She turned to write a couple of notes on my forms. Then she paused to look at the door. A somber expression fell over her face, and I wondered if she was thinking about what had upset Atticus so badly. "My job requires that I reveal your identity to the Court, which I'll be doing as soon as I leave. They are pretty strict about knowing who and what is walking our streets. Just in case anyone decides to cause trouble. I'm also supposed to tell you your species if you are unaware, which I'll admit is a rarity." She paused, giving me a once-over. "But I suspect you'll be figuring that out much sooner than you think all on your own. Good luck, Ember."

That was it.

I wished that she would say more. Anything that would clear away the clutter in my mind. Instead, she just smiled and turned away. I hesitated, hoping that she would add something else, but it became obvious that she was done. She really was refusing to tell me the truth. A truth that I apparently wasn't ready to accept. Whatever the heck that meant.

Turning the door handle, I opened the door but paused to turn back.

"Thank you for this." I held up my tattoo. "I can't explain it, but I feel somehow more at peace now."

She offered me a weak smile. "I'm glad. And I hope you find what you're looking for. Just keep an open mind. Not everything is black and white. Sometimes it's the gray areas where we find ourselves."

I nodded my head in farewell and stepped through the door. The waiting room was empty.

"Atticus must be waiting outside." I hated that I'd somehow upset him. But it would be a lie to deny the feeling I got when I realized he'd seen my tattoo come to life. Did that have something to do with our growing attraction? Was there some sort of a bond that we shared?

"Ember!"

I turned back to see Addie running toward me. Her gaze flitted around the empty room before she leaned in close.

"I know why you're here in Havenwood Falls," she said in a rush. "The man you're looking for is called Mehki."

"What?" I blinked, shocked. "How did you—"

She clasped her hand over my arm, and I felt my tattoo begin to grow warm. "I can't tell you any more than that. Just watch your back. This town may seem nice enough, but there are plenty of ears listening."

"Wait, Addie!" But she turned and ran back the way she came. When she reached the doorway to the room where I'd received my tattoo, she ran through.

"Mehki," I whispered, staring at the wall across from me. I finally knew the name of my momma's killer. "I'm coming for you."

CHAPTER 10

I found Atticus waiting for me next to his Subaru, his hands shoved deep into his jeans. He was staring at the dormant ski lift that rose up the mountain, but I doubted he saw it.

"Want to tell me what that was all about?" I asked. He didn't react when I walked up.

"Nope."

"You've done nothing but dig into my business since we met. And the one time I ask you a question, all you can say is nope?" Crossing my arms over my chest, I shook my head. "That's not how this works. You asked me to trust you, and I told you things no one else has ever heard before. So it's time you start talking. Trust goes both ways, buddy."

It was true that I'd extended a bit of trust to him this morning. Beyond that, he was on a need-to-know basis. Anything more, and I might have to kill him.

When he turned to look at me, I faltered. There was an emptiness in his gaze that made my heart seize up. An irrational desire to wrap him in my arms and tell him that everything would be okay gripped me. I knew that pain all too well. It was the sort that only came from death. One you felt guilty about, at that.

"You want to know the truth? Fine." When he looked down at the tattoo on my arm, his lip turned up into a sneer. "One of those killed my parents."

"A phoenix?" This time I stepped back. "How?"

Atticus looked back to the mountains. "About six months ago, my mom and dad went on a trip to Denver for their anniversary. I guess they stayed longer than they'd planned and were coming back well after midnight. Had a few extra drinks on top, I'm sure. My dad always did like a good whiskey." A muscle flexed in his jaw as he paused to rein in his emotions. "The attack happened on their way home."

His words didn't feel right. From what little I knew about phoenixes, they seemed like gentle creatures. The lore claimed they loved nature and its creation. I couldn't imagine one attacking someone. Heck, I couldn't imagine one actually being alive, for that matter. They were supposed to be extremely rare.

"What happened?" I asked.

He blew out a breath. "I was out of town when it happened. My brother, Orlon, had sent me after a shipment of fertilizer. On the way back, my truck blew a tire. Normally I would have changed it and gone on, but we had removed the spare to make extra space for the bags. I had to sleep in the truck until the tow company opened. When Joshua Breen came to tow me back to town the next morning, he told me they were gone."

"And no one tried to call you?"

"Sure they did. Trouble is, some of these mountain passes have a crap signal. Had to climb halfway up the mountain to get through."

Maybe that's why Havenwood Falls didn't show on my GPS. Atticus would blame it on the mystical force or some crap like that.

"Did anyone see the accident?"

"No."

I frowned. "Well, maybe the secondhand account got it wrong? I've spent my fair share of time in jail for disorderly conduct or other lame complaints filed against me. No two people ever see an event in the same light."

"It was a phoenix. I know it was."

I didn't want to press him too hard, but I needed to know more. "How?"

"My uncle said he saw it. Like a huge fireball shooting across the sky. He's always been fascinated with phoenix lore. Used to talk to me about it when I was a kid. Back then, he made it sound so magical and elusive. A creature of immense beauty and power that could live for hundreds of years, and then begin again." He shook his head. "I think it was the immortality aspect of the bird that fascinated him so much. That and its healing powers."

I blinked. "Can a phoenix heal itself?"

"Maybe. How else could it live so long? That's not so hard to believe. Many of us supes have that ability. But the phoenix is different. It can cheat death using its tears. There's a special kind of magic hidden there. But it does have one enemy. A roc."

I had a vague memory of reading about this giant bird from my studies. It made me wonder about the bird I'd seen soaring over the valley the night I arrived. Was it a roc? It was certainly big enough to be one, but it had looked too peaceful to be a killer. But looks were always deceiving.

"And that was all important to your uncle?" I asked.

Atticus frowned at my probing question. "He has his reasons."

When he went silent, I knew not to push the issue. But I had a gazillion questions racing through my mind when he did choose to speak again.

"When he saw that bird lit against the night sky, he took off to follow it. I guess he thought if he could capture a picture of it, then it would be real to people. Kinda like how some folks hunt Bigfoot, like Sherman. They need proof."

I could understand that. Legends and lore were rooted in cultures across the world. People liked to consider the "what if" of their reality. Most, if they knew the real truth, were better off staying in the dark.

"My uncle saw the explosion on the mountainside. He hurried to reach the spot, but when he arrived . . ." Atticus paused to carve his fingers through his hair. When he spoke again, there was a quake in his voice. "I don't know why that bird chose my parents as its target. They were good people. Kind and generous to everyone they met. The only thing remaining from their car was the license plate. It tore off when they crashed into the tree."

"What about the car? There had to be something left of it," I asked, thinking back to the molten heap of metal that I'd turned that Rolls Royce back in Denver into. Sure, it'd burned, but there still something left.

"Nothing. Not even a single tire skid mark. I guess the blaze burned away the evidence."

The feeling of unease continued, but I didn't speak of it. It wasn't my place to contradict his story further or to insert my own personal feelings into it. But in my gut, I knew something was off.

"And the bird?" I held my breath, torn between feeling sorry for his loss and desperate to know what happened to the phoenix.

"Gone." His voice lost all emotion. "Sheriff Kasun was the first on the scene. He told me later that they found claw marks high in the trees after they sniffed around for a bit. That bird must have perched up high to watch my uncle fall apart over losing his kin."

A tremble began to spread through me as I let that imagery sink in. It ran far too parallel to what my momma's killer did. It was terrible to imagine another creature being so cold and heartless.

Addie's earlier comments about his brother Orlon's heavy drinking started to make sense. The man was trying to drown out his pain. That was another thing I knew about. But I used fighting to release the bitterness.

"And your brother? Was he here when it happened?"

"No. He was on a date. The last one he may ever have, thanks to this." Atticus shook his head. "He's really torn up about it. Blames himself, not that there was anything he could have done."

"And you?" I reached out and placed a hand on his arm. The instant we connected, I felt my tattoo come to life again, but I ignored it.

He turned to look at me. A sad, heartbreaking smile touched his lips as he placed his hand on mine. "I keep telling myself that if I ever find that bird, I'll gut it for what it did to my parents. But guys like me never get that chance. I'm no hunter like you. Havenwood Falls is my home. I doubt that phoenix would dare come back again."

It was hard for me to offer condolences when it felt like a betrayal to even speak the words.

"Besides," he said with a forced a smile, "if there's a way I can help you avenge your mom's death, it might help me find peace, too."

"So that's why you've been such a pain?" I laughed, trying to lift the mood. "You're using me as a distraction?"

A flicker of some unspoken emotion flashed across his face, and my breath caught. In that split second, heat swirled in my hands, and I knew I could lose control with him. But the emotion vanished just as quickly as it came, and the heat faded.

"Nothing wrong with a good distraction now and then." He winked.

Clearing my throat, I stepped back to put some much-needed space between us. "I may have a new clue for us to go on. Feel up to doing some digging?"

"Yeah, I am." His smile returned. It didn't reach its full charm, but it was a far cry better than his earlier hollowness. "Point me in the right direction and I'll—"

Before he could finish his sentence, his hand slammed into my chest and shoved me backward. I landed hard on the concrete, my tailbone cursing his name before I could get back to my feet.

"What the—"

"Sheriff Kasun," Atticus called. He waved at the driver of the unmarked black Chevy truck pulling into a parking spot a few feet away. Atticus rounded the front of his SUV. "Nice to see you."

Hurrying toward the driver's side tire on his Subaru, I pulled my legs tight into my chest.

"Atticus." The cop's boots ground against the rocks lining the edge of the road, fallen from the landscaped path. Ducking my head to look under the car, I was surprised to see the sheriff decked out in casual attire. "Don't you mow the cemetery on Sundays?"

"Sure do." Atticus leaned back against his car across from where I crouched. He probably thought he was helping to hide me. If anything, he'd drawn the cop's eyes to my location. "I needed to take a day off. Been working too hard lately. Addie mentioned that Orlon hit the tavern pretty hard last night. Thought it might be a good idea to stick around town in case he needs anything."

"Tate mentioned seeing him in there. Said he looked a bit rough." There was a long pause, broken by the cop clearing his throat. "I'm sorry about your parents, Atticus. Not sure I ever got around to saying that, what with the investigation and all. Wish we had more to go on."

"The town and your family keep you busy. I know that, Ric."

I closed my eyes, hating that the sheriff had dredged up those feelings again. Atticus at least sounded more in control now.

"Is there anything I can do for you, Sheriff, or are you passing through?"

"I was on my way out to your cabin to talk to you. Found a stolen car abandoned in town yesterday with a new girl passing through. Lloyd mentioned that the girl clipped you. Hinted that you'd taken a liking to her and decided not to press charges. I'd like to have a chat with her."

I heard Atticus scratch at the stubble on his cheek. "Is she in some kind of trouble?"

"Well, that depends on how she came to be in that car. Lloyd seems to think she stole it."

"And you?"

The sheriff shifted his footing. "Her scent was all over the vehicle, as were her prints, but that makes sense if she was sleeping in it. We're waiting for the report to get back on the car's registration. You know how things are after the Midsummer Night's mess. It's hard to get people focused again."

"I bet last night kept you busy."

"Yes." His disgruntled agreement almost made me smile. I could only imagine the things people got up to.

"Thinking about it, maybe she found the car abandoned and needed a place to crash. It wouldn't be the first time that's happened around here."

"You always were too positive to be a cop, Atticus," Ric said. "If you see the girl, let her know I'm looking for her. I've got Tate and Conall sniffing around, too."

That was the second time he'd mentioned using scent to track me. Lifting my face, I did a bit of sniffing myself and caught the distinct scent of dog.

Ugh. I hated wolf shifters. Especially when they had my scent to track. That made them hard to evade. Thankfully, the cloud of ozone-killing crap coming out of Atticus's muffler was probably enough to keep me hidden.

"Good to know," Atticus said, pushing off the car to shake hands with the cop.

I held my breath as the sheriff returned to his truck. The man did a three-point turn and headed in the opposite direction. Atticus waited until the Chevy disappeared before he rounded the car. "Did I hurt you?"

"Nothing a hot bath wouldn't cure." I winced, rubbing the throbbing in my hip where Fluffy's bruise was still healing.

He offered a hand. "I can arrange that."

"Atticus?" I said, stopping him before he moved to open my car door. "Thank you."

"For what?"

"For covering for me back there. You didn't have to. I know I'm putting you in a bind with the people around here, and I just . . ." I rubbed the back of my neck. "Thanks."

He smiled. "I'm a nice guy, remember?"

The ride back to his cabin was silent. I slumped in his front seat in case one of Kasun's men spotted me. We didn't talk about the wolf pack or the fact that Atticus was going to be watched over the next few days. Whatever hopes he had of trying to help me had gone out the window. I wasn't going to let my presence cause him any more trouble than it already had.

"Go on inside and start the fire. There's kindling and wood next to the stove. I'll bring some water from the stream." He put the car in park when we arrived at his front door.

I looked all around. "I don't see any water."

"It's a bit farther down the mountain. The hike sounds worse than it is." He came around to open my door, but I sat there staring up at him. "What?"

"I can't figure you out." And believe me, I was trying. Every time I turned around, he did something sweet and totally unexpected. I'd been around strangers for so long that I had become accustomed to callous looks or snide remarks. But Atticus was different.

"So I'm a man of mystery?" He rubbed his chin and nodded. "I can live with that."

I laughed. "I'm serious. What sort of man offers to haul heavy tubs of water halfway up a mountain just for a complete stranger to take a bath?"

"The sort that wants to see you in his Led Zeppelin shirt again." He winked, then grabbed two large buckets off the front porch and headed away. There was a little extra swagger in his walk that I couldn't help but appreciate.

As I watched him disappear, I chuckled to myself. "A guy like that could make leaving Havenwood Falls a hard thing to do."

Turning to shove open the unlocked door to Atticus's cabin, I saw movement from the corner of my eye. A figure emerged from behind a tree. He stood as tall as Atticus, but had more of a lean build. Ropes of muscle lined his bare arms. His beard held a reddish tint as he stepped into the sun. The resemblance to Atticus was striking.

"Orlon? You're Atticus's brother, right?" I said. "He went to get some water and will be . . ."

"So it is true." His hands clenched into tight fists, still wrapped in leather work gloves. There was a crazed look in his eye as he stared at my phoenix tattoo. "You killed my parents!"

I was so shocked by his accusation that I didn't react until he'd closed the gap and circled his hands around my neck. A garbled cry burst from my lips when he squeezed. I beat at his hands and brought my knee into his groin. The reflex to the pain loosened his grip enough for me to break free. But Orlon tackled me from behind with enough force to send us toppling over the porch railing.

The instant I landed, I jabbed my elbow into his side and scrambled to my feet. "Atticus!"

I clenched my fists to keep my flames contained. I didn't want to hurt Orlon. He was confused, desperate to find someone to blame. I couldn't fault him for that, but I also couldn't let him hurt me.

Orlon snagged a handful of my hair and yanked me to the ground. I screamed and fought back, twisting around to rake my nails across his face. My cheek exploded in pain at his backhand, and several strands of hair ripped free.

"Don't make me hurt you," I warned. The tingling increased, the flames begging to be free.

"I knew one of these days you'd come back to gloat." Spittle hit my cheek as he growled into my ear.

"Orlon, I know you're hurting and this feels right, but I'm not who you think I am."

He yanked me to my feet and slammed my face into the car window. The glass spiderwebbed under the impact. My temple was sliced open, and blood trickled down my face. Darkness edged my vision as I fought against the need to let it take me. "Don't you say my name!"

The man was beyond reasoning with, but I had to try. I'd been where he was. I didn't want him to make the same mistakes.

"Please," I struggled to say around the rapid swelling of my split lip. I tasted blood. "Don't do this."

"Is that what my mom said before you lit her up?" He pressed his body against mine. I blinked back the tears as the barrel of a gun pressed against my back. When it nestled into my spine, sheer panic hit me. He was too blind to see the truth.

"You've got the wrong girl. I swear. I've never been to Havenwood Falls before."

With a growl, he whipped me around to face him. "You expect me to trust you? A murderer?"

I closed my eyes. The heat in my palms had reached excruciating levels, even for me. My body had begun to tremble. "Orlon, stop! I'm warning you."

He pressed the gun to my abdomen. "I know a few things about your kind. About how you can heal all wounds. How death is laughable to you when you've got centuries spread out before you, but I'm an excellent shot. All it takes is one little bullet to immobilize you. A spinal wound would take a bit to heal. I reckon I've got a place I can hide you away to make sure no one finds you again."

"You want to kill me?"

He laughed. "Oh, no. There's someone you need to meet first. I just need to keep you from finding a way to escape."

"What about Atticus?" I needed to keep him talking. Atticus had to be back soon with the water. Maybe he could talk sense to his brother before this escalated.

Orlon spat to the side. "If he knew what I know about you, he'd have done the same thing when he first met you."

My breath caught. He was right. I'd seen the rage that lingered beneath Atticus's calm exterior at the sight of my tattoo. He may not have been drinking away his sorrows at the local tavern, but he was far from handling his parents' deaths well.

"Filthy phoenix," Orlon spat at me and twisted us around so that he was pressed against the car, giving him extra leverage. "I'll kill you for what you did."

The firebird on my forearm fluttered its wings. The tingling from my hand traveled up to my heart, spilling liquid flames into my chest.

What if I am a phoenix? Addie told me that I already knew, that my tattoo was meant for me. And Atticus said that a phoenix had healing tears. Not to mention I was drawn to fire. But I couldn't be. I wasn't thousands of years old. Heck, I wasn't a bird at all.

"Any final words?" Orlon's breath reeked of cheap whiskey as he leered at me.

"Yeah." I focused on his glazed eyes and knew I had no choice. A thirst for murder had darkened his heart. It was a perfect reflection of my own. "Screw you."

Orlon pulled back as I opened my hands. A brilliant glow of flames burst between us, sending him flying back through the air. The impact crumpled the hood of Atticus's Subaru. I landed on my hands and knees, dazed by the intensity of the explosion. It made my head swim and my stomach clench with nausea.

"Whoa." I shook my head to clear it. "Never felt that before."

The ground around me was scorched black. The last of the flames died out when I trampled over them in a dead sprint in the direction Atticus went. He hadn't been clear on how far that stream was.

"Get back here!"

A bullet whizzed past my head. I screamed and ducked, veering onto a new course. A second bullet grazed my cheek, but I kept going. Pumping my arms and legs, I headed straight for the downslope only to realize that it wasn't a slope at all. It was a cliff.

"No!" My scream echoed around me as I tried to slow my momentum, but it was too late. I slid right off the edge and fell.

CHAPTER 11

*T*he wind whipped my hair into a frenzy as I plummeted from the cliff. Bits of dirt crumbled at the edge and pelted me. My heart clenched at the sight of the ground rushing up to meet me.

This was it. The moment my life should be flashing before my eyes, but all I could see was Atticus. How freaking annoying was that? I could have at least spent my last seconds on this earth thinking of something great. Like the saltwater taffy my momma used to buy me, or one of her hugs.

Instead, the image of Atticus's lopsided grin actually made me smile. The fact that I was about to splatter all over the rocks below didn't seem quite so terrifying.

"Oomph." I crashed into something soft and warm, and my eyes flew open. Instead of the ground being on swift approach, the sun was. All around me, the soft down of feathers flapped as a great bird carried me into the heavens. "Holy—!"

Terror seized me as the bird took a steep ascent. I gripped onto its neck with all my might. It rose higher, and the air became cold and thin. I buried my face in its back, willing my heart to not give out on me from shock.

"This can't be happening," I whispered as the bird dipped and swooped, gliding with grace on the wind. My teeth stopped chattering as we sank back toward the earth.

Daring to open my eyes again, I saw the trees passing by at

frightening speeds mere inches from the bird's belly. The force of the wind dried out my eyes, but I couldn't look away.

"It's beautiful," I said, staring in awe.

I felt a great rumble in the bird's breast before it released a bone-rattling cry. It rotated its head so that its eye watched me.

"Did you just agree with me?"

Its head bobbed, and I laughed. That's when I noticed the fine white lines that traced through amber and chestnut tones on the crown of its head. "Atticus? Holy crap. Is that you?"

I eased off my death grip and sat back. I was safe with him. Also a bit mortified that I'd needed him to save me. Lord, what I must have looked like as I fell!

"I knew you were a shifter all along," I announced. This time the rumbling from beneath my arms was a laugh.

The view was breathtaking. The mountains stretched out before us. With two powerful flaps of his wings, Atticus shot straight for them. Then he spiraled into a dive just before we hit.

I laughed and threw out my hands on either side as he leveled. "Show-off!"

As we glided back toward Atticus's house, I remembered why I'd needed saving in the first place.

"Oh! Atticus." I leaned down to speak where I thought his ear might be. "Your brother was there, at your cabin. I don't know how to say this, but he attacked me. That's why I went over the cliff."

The bird trembled beneath me.

"I'm so sorry. I should have told you sooner. Orlon—" My words cut off as Atticus suddenly dove to the ground. He pulled up at the last second, folded his wings and glided to a stop in front of the cabin.

Dipping his wing, he allowed me to slide to the ground. I cast a wary glance at the forest but saw no movement. Atticus's bird eye followed my gaze.

"I'm sorry," I whispered. It was a little unnerving talking to a giant bird. "He wasn't thinking straight. He saw my tattoo and thought . . ."

He dropped his head.

"Sorry about your car." I glanced at the extensive damage. "I'll pay you back for the damages."

He flapped his wings in agitation. The great gust sent me sprawling to the ground.

"This would be a lot easier if you were human again," I muttered, bracing myself in case he decided to flap again. I'd spent far too much time already having my backside handed to me today.

With a small twitch of his wing, I got a distinct impression that he wanted me to turn around.

"Let me guess, you're naked after you shift, aren't you?" The temptation to turn around and check him out was strong, but I resisted out of respect to him.

When he pressed his chest against my back, I chuckled at the obvious answer. "I guess I asked for that one."

"You could be naked too if you wanted."

There he went with that whole "if I want" thing. If there was ever a more loaded question to answer, I sure didn't know what it was.

"Nice to see you still have your sense of humor. Does that mean I'm forgiven for your car?"

Atticus went rigid behind me. For a moment he didn't speak. I wanted to, but wasn't sure what to say. "I'm sorry about my brother. I know Addie's tattoo put me in a bad headspace, but she should've known how you sporting that tattoo would make our family feel. It hasn't been easy for us. The wounds are still raw. But if I'd thought that Orlon would . . ."

"Hey." I eased around to face him but kept my eyes chest height and above. It didn't seem right to check out his junk without permission. Though I got the feeling that he was testing me to see if I would. "It's okay. I'm a big girl. I can take care of myself."

"Says the girl who tossed herself off a cliff!"

I laughed and nodded. "Okay, that might not have been my best move, but to be fair, I was being shot at."

"My brother shot at you?" Atticus blinked, trying to process it all. That's when he noticed the healing mark on my cheek. He cupped his hand around my neck and pulled me close. "I'm so sorry he hurt you."

"It's just a scratch."

"It could've been so much more. Orlon is a skilled marksman, Ember. He never misses his target."

"Well, I guess I got lucky then."

Or that concussion I gave him screwed with his aim a bit. I kept that thought to myself.

I shuddered as he wrapped his arms around me. Never before had I felt such a strong burst of power. What happened between Orlon and me was more than a usual flame. It had been electric. My arms still ached from where they shook with effort as I tried to hold it back for so long.

Something was changing inside of me. I could feel an energy pulsating.

"Are you okay?" He pulled back to look down at me.

I started to give him the obligatory response but stopped myself. Atticus cared. He deserved more than that.

"He thinks I'm the one who killed your parents."

"I assumed as much." Atticus winced. "I thought the same thing when I saw your tattoo."

That admission stung more than I wanted it to.

"You know I'd never . . . I couldn't . . ." But I didn't finish that statement because I knew that I could. I'd killed before. Not without reason, but the stain of death was on my hands.

"Of course not." He tucked my head into his chest again. "Orlon needs someone to blame. You're an outsider bearing the wrong mark. I should have anticipated how he might react."

But it didn't feel like the wrong mark. In fact, it was the total opposite. For the first time in my life, something felt right.

"It's not your fault." I leaned up to kiss him on the cheek but froze. Where his cheek touched my lips, a warm tingle began.

Now, I wasn't the swoony romantic sort, but there was no denying this physical reaction. It was like the initial tingling in my palms before the ball of fire would appear. Kissing Atticus's cheek resonated within whatever part of my soul connected me to the flames.

Whoa.

"Did you feel that?" I whispered.

Atticus cleared his throat. When his hands settled on my hips, I realized that he was still very naked and there wasn't a sliver of space between us. "Yep. Pretty sure I'm feeling something."

I laughed and slapped him on the arm. "Way to ruin the moment."

"That's what you wanted, right?" He stared at me with a sudden intensity that I felt both drawn to and terrified of. I was getting in over my head, and he was trying to give me an out.

"Sure." I shrugged and kept my eyes fixed on his until I'd turned around and it was safe to look down. "You should probably find some pants."

"I'll be back in a minute. I want to check things out. Make sure Orlon is gone."

"And if he's not?" I asked, wrapping my arms around myself.

"I'm not going anywhere tonight. I promise I'll never let him hurt you again."

As he shifted back into the great bird and took to the sky, I sighed. "But what if I hurt you?"

WE ATE dinner in silence a few hours later. Both of us were lost in our thoughts. Atticus's search hadn't turned up anything. Orlon was gone, but I knew he would be back. And this time, I wouldn't hold back. He'd threatened my life. No amount of grief could excuse that.

I didn't tell Atticus how close his brother had come to paralyzing me. Laying that guilt on him wasn't something he needed. By the droop of his shoulders, he was already placing enough guilt on himself for the both of us. It would seem the blame game was a family trait.

I barely tasted the fillet of fish and roasted broccoli that I pushed around my plate. The scent of butter and herbs lingered in the air. Under normal circumstances I would have been thrilled with his cooking skills, but not tonight. All the same, I made sure to thank Atticus for the effort he put into making it for me. After we cleaned the dishes together, I moved to stand at the glass doors and stared out at the valley. Havenwood Falls disappeared as the shadows grew longer and night claimed the sky.

A shiver ran down my spine.

"You okay?" Atticus stood behind me, close enough for me to feel safe.

"Yes," I said in a whisper. "And no."

"Do you want to talk about it?"

I turned to look at him. His face was lost to shadow, but I could see the golden glow of his eyes. The same glow I'd seen before.

"It was you that I saw flying the night I arrived in town, wasn't it?"

"That was you in the car?" He laughed and moved toward the couch. "Sorry if I scared you. I didn't expect to see anyone on the road so late and cut the curve closer than I should have."

I sank next to him, my knee touching his side. The loveseat's oversized cushions pressed us closer together. "Have you always known that you're a giant bird?"

He shifted to face me. "Yeah, I guess. I mean, my whole family is, so you sort of grow up knowing that someday you'll be like them."

"When was your first time?"

He arched an eyebrow at that, and I laughed. "I'm trying to have a serious conversation, and your mind is in the gutter."

"Sorry," he muttered and lowered his gaze. I was wearing his favorite T-shirt again. The hunger I saw in his gaze each time he looked at me was starting to become mine as well. "I guess it was when I was a teenager. Maybe a bit earlier. My brother was older and a bit of a know-it-all. Orlon used to taunt me about having his wings long before I did. One night, he coaxed me into jumping off City Hall."

"What happened?"

Atticus shot me a sheepish grin and rubbed his hand down his left leg. "I broke a few ribs, this knee and shattered one arm. But the second time I flew."

I laughed. Despite my encounter with Orlon, I liked the way Atticus talked about his brother. Sibling rivalry was something I'd always seen but never experienced. Rivalry in foster homes was totally different.

"Mom wanted to clip his wings over that one, let me tell you." There was a note of sadness in his voice at the memory. "You would've liked her. She was one of those people that lit up the room. Always ready with a quick joke or to lend a hand to someone in need."

"I see where you get it from. Always the giver, even when it's annoying." I smiled.

His eyes grew wide for a second, but then he laughed. "Yeah, I guess you're right. I never really thought about it much. What about you? Are you anything like your mom?"

I lowered my gaze. The skin around my nails was raw and bleeding from when I'd tried to stop my fall.

"I don't remember much. After Momma died in the fire, I went to a few doctors. Some tended to my burns, but the others wanted to dig through my brain." I didn't expand on that, because to do so would be to admit that there had been a time that even I thought I was crazy. "There was one man who was kind. Dr. Darcy tried to explain to me that sometimes when a child undergoes a traumatic event, the mind shuts down. Sometimes it does that by splintering off pieces of memory. Then it shoves them into some locked box in the back of your mind."

"Sure." He nodded. "It's a way of protecting yourself."

"Exactly. Dr. Darcy believed there were strings of events that got all tangled up in my head. Like that game kids sometimes play where you hold a string and wind through the big tangle to try to find the end. Well, he said I was still trying to find my ending and that's why my memories are all jumbled up."

Atticus laid a comforting hand on mine. "So you don't remember anything?"

"Sometimes I get these flashes of images. Like a scent will trigger a memory. Or a place will feel familiar. I remember my momma's smile most of all." I lifted my gaze. His tender smile broke through whatever defenses I thought I still had against this man. "I don't think about her much. It's easier not to."

"Hey." He pushed in closer to me and rested his hands on my shoulders. "I understand. Believe me, I do. There were days when I didn't want to get out of bed, or wondered if I'd ever laugh again. I felt guilty when something good happened, because it was a reminder of what my parents missed out on. That they'd never get the chance to experience joy again. I feel that way with you."

I turned away to wipe at my eyes. "You do?"

"Ember." His breath washed over my cheek. He was so close now. "I know life hasn't been easy for you. I can see it in the way you carry yourself. You push everyone away so you don't have to feel. I get it. But I swear to you that I would never do anything to hurt you."

I wanted to believe him.

"I'm here for you. No matter what."

A part of me wanted to laugh, crack some joke about how sappy he was being, but I knew he meant every word of it. That scared the ever-loving crap out of me.

I wasn't ready to fall for a guy. Least of all one I could hurt. What if I was a phoenix? How could he ever look me in the eye without wondering? Without condemning?

"Atticus, I—" He stopped me with a kiss. It happened so fast, I barely realized that his arms had come around me and drawn me into him.

The kiss wasn't filled with heat, but instead tenderness, as his lips moved against mine. I stared at his closed eyes, shocked by how right this felt. I never kissed with my eyes open. Heck, I never kissed, period. It was too personal.

But with Atticus . . . I wanted to.

"Sorry," he whispered when he finally pulled back and opened his eyes. "You looked like you needed that before you went full tilt logic on me. Sometimes letting go is the only way to heal."

"Letting go can be dangerous, too," I countered. He'd left me breathless and a tingling mess. The sensation wasn't limited to my hands now. The electrical charge reached my toes. It wound around my belly and straight up to the tip of my nose. I'd never felt so alive before.

He smiled. "Not if you do it with the right person."

"And you think you're that guy for me?"

Cupping my face, he drew me close again. His gaze lingered on my lips before his lopsided grin drew me in. "There's only one way to find out."

CHAPTER 12

The candlelight flickered from the main living area below. I focused on the shadows they cast on the ceiling as Atticus pressed his lips to the hollow of my throat. His breathing grew ragged, like my own, as I traced my nails along his back. My legs felt weak as he hovered over me.

The neck of his shirt hung low, giving me a teasing hint of what lay beneath. He flinched when I ran my hands up under his shirt but soon settled into my touch. The planes of his stomach were rigid, rippled with muscle that came from years of manual labor.

His fiery kiss ran along my shoulder then back up toward my ear. A low moan rose from my parted lips when he tugged my earlobe between his teeth. His hot breath washed over me. Goosebumps raced down my body beneath the kneading touch of his hands as he gripped my waist.

The hem of my shirt rose high enough for him to explore the length of my angel scar. I wondered if he would see the scar in its entirety before the night was over. Or if I wanted him to.

"Ember," he whispered against my lips.

I closed my eyes to the sensations hearing him speak my name lit in me. His voice was deep, sultry. I wanted him more than I'd ever wanted another man, but I felt his restraint.

"We shouldn't—"

I cut off his words with a kiss, plunging my hands into his hair to hold him close. I wasn't ready for reason to return. If given the choice, I'd rather stay here, in his arms, the whole night through. Here was safe and warm. So very warm.

I lengthened the kiss until our lips were bruised and I panted for breath, but still, it wasn't enough. He tasted of mint. He smelled of fresh dew on grass and flowers newly budded on a spring morning. I couldn't get enough of him.

"Don't," I whispered, breaking the kiss only long enough to breathe.

His eyes were tender as he held my face in his hands. The calluses along his palm brushed against my cheeks as he leaned in for another kiss. This one was soft and gentle. "You know I want to, right?"

I nodded. I could see the truth of his desire burning in the depths of his eyes.

This man could be the end of me. I stared back, memorizing every detail of this moment. From the sheen of sweat on his brow to the flare of his hips encased in jeans.

"I don't want to take advantage of you when you're feeling vulnerable," he said and eased back.

I loved the way the white highlights in his hair seemed to glow in the moonlight. Now I knew they were a part of his feather pattern, soft and beautiful. But there was also a reminder of the events earlier in the day.

"You think this is about your brother?" I asked. He cut his gaze to the side to look out the window, but I reached up and pulled his chin back around to look at me. "Atticus, I didn't kiss you because I'm scared. I kissed you because . . ."

"What?" He propped himself above me so that his weight didn't crush me.

"Nothing," I rushed to say. "Never mind."

"Ember." He brushed my hair back from my face. "Sweet, beautiful Ember. It's okay to admit that you are hopelessly attracted to me. I know I'm irresistible."

I burst out laughing and yanked him back down to me. Our lips crashed together, but I didn't care that he'd smashed my nose or that it was hard to breathe under his big frame. All that mattered was his taste, the feel of him against me, and the obvious press of his need against my thigh.

With each moment that he consumed my lips, the temperature in the room rose. Kicking his bent knee out from under him, I rolled until I was on top. His hands settled on my waist. His eyes drifted low to take in my exposed thighs.

"I didn't think you could look any more beautiful, but I was wrong."

I smiled down at him before I leaned in to take his lower lip between my teeth. He inhaled sharply. Reaching up, I took hold of his wrists and placed them over his head. Holding them with one hand, I explored his stomach with the other.

"I'd say the same to you," I teased, trailing my fingers through the soft hair that led into his waistband. "But it would just go to your head."

He groaned when I moved my hand higher. "You're doing that on purpose."

"Of course I am."

He resisted my hold as I licked along his jaw. Heat swelled around us as I teased and taunted him. Steam fogged up the windows. I explored his chest and nipped at his neck. His fingers tugged against my grasp as he tried to remain in control. Ever the gentleman, though I could feel how much he wished he could give in.

The sheets lay crumpled beneath him. His head pressed tight against the pillow, teeth buried in his lower lip as I ground my hips against him. His body was taut with need. I knew that it wouldn't take much more to weaken his resolve.

When I released him and his hand fell to the side of my hip, I couldn't help but flinch in response. Atticus went still.

"Are you hurt?"

"Don't stop," I said, but he was already shifting to try to look.

"Holy—" He rolled me off. When his hand lifted the hem of my shirt, I closed my eyes. I knew what he saw. Fluffy's bite mark had sealed over, but the bruise was still extensive and ugly. "Who did this to you?"

I sighed and yanked the shirt out of his hand. "The question you should be asking is what did this to me. It was a skinwalker. That snitch I told you about wasn't human."

Atticus's eyes bulged. "You're lying."

"Nope." I shoved my hair back out of my face. "Kinda wish I was, though. His teeth were sharp."

He stared at me for a minute. Long enough for me to wonder if I'd suddenly sprouted three heads of my own.

"Who are you?" he said.

Realizing that any hope of time spent with him under the sheets had vanished, I slipped to the edge of the bed. "I told you already."

"Well, you failed to mention this little bit of information about facing off with a skinwalker."

My skin felt clammy when I ran my hands along my arms. It was way too hot in here.

"Kinda like you forgot to mention that you're a giant bird," I said.

He raised his hands in defense. "That's fair. I did. But you can't drop a bomb like this on me and not say more. How did you run into a skinwalker?"

I shrugged. "It was a fight club in Denver."

"A fight club." He laughed and shook his head. "Of course it was. Because that's something normal people do."

I narrowed my eyes at him. "I never claimed to be normal."

"No. In fact, I'm starting to realize that you're anything but." The heat under his gaze became stifling. "First you take on a skinwalker, which is insane, by the way. Then you steal a car, which I helped cover for you, so now I'm involved. You're here to find your mom's killer. I'm assuming you don't intend to give him a slap on his wrist and send him on his way. This means I may end up an accessory to murder. You've already told me that you've been in and out of trouble your whole life."

"So?"

Atticus looked taken aback. "Doesn't any of that bother you?"

I frowned. "What choice did I have? This is the life I was handed."

"It doesn't have to be." He turned to face me fully. I tried not to notice how his shirt had ridden up. The sight of his glorious abs was a distraction. "You can start over here."

"What? With you? Is that what you were going to say?" I laughed. "Who are we kidding, Atticus? Your brother wants me dead. The sheriff is after me. And as soon as I do track down my momma's killer, I'm going to take him out one way or another. So whatever you think we have between us . . . don't. You're better off without me in your life."

"What if I don't want to be? Out of your life, I mean?"

I pushed up to my feet. "This was a mistake. I have a rule: don't get close to anyone."

"Wow." He shook his head. "I think I understand now. That chip on your shoulder is to make sure you don't care about anyone but yourself."

"Whatever." I didn't like how close he'd come to pegging me. There was more to it than that. There had to be.

"Ember." Atticus grabbed hold of my arm when I tried to move toward the ladder.

"Don't!" But it was too late. Shimmering light consumed my firebird tattoo a split second before two fireballs burst from my palms. One lit the hem of the bedding. The second brushed past his arm and set his shirt on fire.

He scrambled back as the flames rose up between his legs, lighting his jeans. He tumbled off the other side. When he got to his feet he began yanking off his clothes until he was down to his boxers.

He stared in wide-eyed disbelief at the damage. Then he looked at where I stood with a pillow in hand over the smothered flames.

"How did you—"

I closed my eyes. "You're really going to have to learn how to finish those sentences."

"But how?" I heard him swallow. I could hear the thundering of his heart in his chest. I could even hear the bead of sweat that fell from his brow and hit the hardwood floor.

"I told you. I'm not normal."

"Did you . . ." He shook his head. "You didn't try to hit me with those fireballs, did you?"

My eyes popped open. "Of course not. I would never."

"Then what happened?"

I didn't know. I knew he wasn't trying to hurt me. Why did I lose control like that? I hadn't even felt the tingling in my hands before.

"Crap." I tugged on a swatch of sweaty hair. "I was hot."

Atticus stared at me.

"It's this thing that happens before I, you know, go all pyro and whatnot." I turned to stare at the charred bedding where I'd lain in his arms only moments ago. "It was you."

"Excuse me?"

I spun to face him. "You're my trigger. Why I lost control. I was so focused on you that I lost myself, and when you grabbed my arm, it must have thrown me into a fight response."

His brow furrowed. "You're blaming this on me?"

"No. That's not what I—" I growled out my frustration. "I'm not making any sense."

"No. And neither is your hair."

"What?" Freaked out by the intensity of his stare, I snatched my hair and gasped. Running my hands through the strands, I saw a wide black streak had formed from near my right eye to the tips. Nothing like that had ever happened before, and I'd wielded fire countless times.

When I looked back at Atticus, I saw he'd backed away. "Atticus?"

"You glowed," he said, his gaze looking beyond me. "Just before you threw the fire at me, it was like your aura caught on fire. Everything burned."

My mouth fell open. I wanted to say something, but the storm clouds darkening his handsome features stopped me.

When his gaze shifted to meet mine, I recoiled. His eyes were far too like those Orlon had glared at me with earlier in the day when he looked down at my tattoo.

"Atticus, I can explain—"

"Is it true?" He cut me off. I tried to cover the bird on my forearm, but heat waves continued to radiate from it. "I think I'm starting to understand now. Addie didn't pull that phoenix tattoo out of thin air, did she? She knew you could control fire."

There was no sense denying the evidence in front of him. "Yes, I can. But this is the first time I've lost control like that."

That wasn't true, though. I'd lost control back in Denver, and it'd cost Fluffy his life.

Atticus began to shake. His fists clenched at his sides. "Why didn't you tell me you could wield fire?"

"Why?" I scoffed and wrapped my arms around myself. Only a moment ago I had felt free in his arms, but now I was a freak. "Because I knew you would look at me like that. With condemnation and hatred in your eyes. Just like your brother!"

The floor creaked when he came to a sudden halt. "You can toss fireballs, Ember. I've never met a supe that can do that!"

"Don't you think I know that?" I yelled back. My voice quaked with anger and frustration. "I have spent my entire life being different from everyone else. God help me, but you made me believe that you might be the first person to overlook that."

Atticus growled and turned away. Every muscle in his back went taut as he fought to control the emotions raging through him.

"Was my brother right about you?"

My arms fell to my sides. "So it's like that, is it? I control fire so that makes me a murderer? Someone you think is capable of killing your parents in cold blood?"

Atticus hung his head. "You just admitted that you're willing to avenge your mom by whatever means necessary. Doesn't that make you capable of that?"

"He took everything from me!" My hands quaked at my sides, and I clenched them for fear of another fire burst.

"So that justifies murder?" he whispered.

I stopped short. If I said yes, that would condemn me, but if I said no, it would be a bald-faced lie.

Atticus slammed his fist into the wall. The wood creaked, and for a moment, I wondered if it might give way. The sheer power of him took me off guard and reminded me that even in his human form he was strong. All this time he'd been holding back with me.

And yet I'm the one condemned for lying. I snorted.

"Fine." I threw up my hands. "If you want to think I'm such a terrible person that I could kill your innocent parents, fine. I can't stop you. But you're wrong, Atticus. I may have had a hard life, and yeah, I've done a few things I'm not proud of, but I would never kill an innocent. And if you want to think I'm a phoenix, well, that's on you. I don't know what I am. I just know that when I'm with you, I feel things that I shouldn't, and it scares me. All of this." I waved my arms at the bed. "That was me. The real me. You said you didn't want to take advantage of me because you thought I was vulnerable. Well, news flash, Atticus. Orlon didn't make me feel vulnerable. You did. That's why I lost control."

With that, I headed for the ladder with every intention of storming off in epic fashion. The trouble was, I forgot that he was a freakin' bird. By the time my foot hit the bottom rung, he'd leaped from the loft and scooped me into his arms.

"Get off me!" I beat at his arm, but he held me with a vise-like grip.

"Where do you think you're going?"

"I still have a murderer to find, remember? That's why I'm here. And if you're done helping me, then I'll find my own way."

A dark glint crossed his eyes. "So that's it? You're just going to run out on me like that?"

"You haven't exactly given me a reason to want to stay." I tried to yank my arm out of his grasp, but he was too strong. "Let me go, Atticus."

"Or what? You'll burn me, too?"

His callous words burrowed deeper than any had before, and I gasped at the sudden stab of pain.

"Of course not. I'd never hurt you. Don't you get that?"

The hard lines of his face softened for a split second, but then firmed up again. "How do I know anything you've said is true?"

"Because I said it's true. That should be enough." A single tear slipped from my eye. He stared at it, appearing as confused as I was by its presence. Then I realized what he saw. The tear shimmered a crimson orange. A tear he would associate with a phoenix.

When he turned and raced for the door, I knew the only way I could get free of his grasp was to burn him, and I would never do that. Not because I promised him I wouldn't. Because I couldn't bear the thought of hurting him.

The instant we were free of the cabin, I felt him beginning to shift. His bones moved, popped, and elongated.

"Where are you taking me?" For the first time, I felt fear.

"To my uncle. Mehki will know if you're lying." His human form shifted away. The giant eagle-like bird stood before me, fierce and beautiful. I could run, but he would catch me.

As I stared into the black of his eyes, I considered the pain to come. Both mine and his. I took my place on his back, knowing that Atticus had no way of knowing his uncle was my momma's killer. But that didn't matter.

Mehki wouldn't live to see the dawn.

CHAPTER 13

I held my breath as the doorbell echoed through the darkened house. If the interior was anything like the extravagant exterior, I knew I'd hate it. The show of wealth didn't fit Atticus's personality or his tiny handmade cabin in the woods. I suspected his uncle had far loftier goals in life.

Atticus's grip on me was just shy of painful as he tapped his foot with impatience. After the third ring, footsteps approached from the other side of the door. Squinting against the sudden brightness of the porch light, I made out the figure of a young girl.

"Atticus?" She sounded sleepy as she rubbed at her eyes. A mess of raven hair fell over her shoulders when she leaned on the doorframe. "You do know that it's like four a.m., right? Now I'll never be awake for my calculus test in the morning."

The girl cut off when she looked at him for the first time. "Why are you naked? And who's the girl you're holding?"

He pushed past her. "Where's Mehki?"

"In bed. Duh." She hurried to follow behind us. It was hard to take in my surroundings when they passed by in a blur of darkness.

"Go and wake him up, Bex. Now!" Atticus left no room for complaint.

A light flicked on, and I found myself carried into a study. Or maybe it was a library. There were enough books lining the shelves to make it one.

"What's your damage?" the girl asked. The uncertain look she shot me was promising. At least, I wanted it to be.

"Bexley, I'm in no mood. Go get your dad."

Never mind. There was no way she was going to be on my side if she was Mehki's daughter.

I half expected Atticus to dump me on the small settee, but instead, he lowered me with care. I refused to meet his gaze, or check out his junk when he stood and began to pace.

"Would you put something on? You already gave your cousin a heart attack showing up like a crazed naked guy in the middle of the night."

"What?" He turned and blinked, appearing confused until he looked down. He crossed his hands to cover himself.

There was nothing in the room that would work in the way of clothing. I saw him look toward the door, but he decided against leaving me alone. That was the first smart thing he'd done all night.

"Use a curtain. Pink flowers suit you." I brought my knees to my chest.

"Cute," he muttered, but did give them a second glance.

"So Mehki's your uncle, huh?" I asked, needing a distraction while we waited. Or at least to make him think I was distracted. I had every intention of being in control when that man walked through the door.

Atticus turned to look at me. "Why?"

"Addie told me about him."

"What? When?" He frowned. "What'd she say?"

I met his gaze. "That he's the one I'm looking for and that I should be careful who I trust. Looks like she was right about one of those so far."

Atticus stopped pacing. "My uncle wouldn't hurt a fly. He's just a normal guy."

"That's what they all say about serial killers," I said under my breath, but knew he heard me when he flinched.

"That's not funny, Ember."

"Not trying to be." I glanced toward the hallway. "Not that it matters. It's pretty obvious you don't trust a word I say."

"That's not . . ." He trailed off, rubbing the back of his head. "I don't know what to think."

"Sure." I nodded as I listened for footsteps. "You know what's funny? Addie must know what your uncle is all about. And yet you stand there, ready to defend a murderer's honor after calling me out for the same thing." I shook my head. "I'm not gonna deny there's irony in that."

He turned and paced a few steps before stopping again. "Addie warned you against me?"

"Well, this whole taking me prisoner thing does kinda make that warning seem legit, doesn't it?"

He swallowed hard and averted his gaze. *Well, I bet that pill sure tasted pretty darn bitter!*

"You're not a prisoner, Ember." He sounded tired. "I just need answers."

"Right. And I gave them to you, but you'd rather think I'm the monster that killed your parents."

He winced at that, refusing to look me in the eye.

"You'd better have a good reason for waking Dad," Bexley said when she entered the room. When she tossed a pair of shorts in Atticus's direction, she didn't notice the tension. Or assumed that it was a normal byproduct of this whole messed up situation. "He's been cranky. I guess his trip to Denver didn't go well."

Atticus paused with one leg in the shorts. "Uncle Mehki was in Denver? I thought he was in Atlanta."

"Yeah. Plans changed, I guess." Bexley sank into the plush seat behind the desk and kept her gaze far from him until he was dressed.

Under the lights she looked pale, her skin taking on an almost jaundiced tint. Now that I really looked, I noticed that the dark circles under her eyes were very pronounced for a teenager. One sniff told me this girl was sick.

"Mom flew into a rage when he showed up in the middle of the night. Even tossed her favorite vase at him."

Atticus frowned and watched me from the corner of his eye. He knew that's where I'd been hunting. "What was he doing in Denver, Bex?"

"How should I know? Dad never talks about family business with me. He thinks I'm too fragile." She scrunched up her nose. As an afterthought, she yanked a box off the bookshelf and pulled out a medical mask. She looped it around her ears. There were several boxes around the room. "Not that I'd care anyway. All that landscaping convention stuff is boring."

I snorted and shook my head. Both sets of eyes turned to look at me. Atticus's demanded an explanation. "What?"

"Are you that blind? A landscaping convention? Please. No one would go to one of those."

Atticus's expression soured. It hurt that he shut me out again, but knowing to expect it this time around made it easier to deal with.

"That's it!" Bexley's outburst from behind her mask startled me as she snapped her fingers. "I knew your girlfriend looked familiar."

"She's not my—" But he cut off as Bexley hurried back through the doorway. "Teenagers."

Atticus slumped into a chair. When he covered his face with his hand, I was grateful to be hidden from him. Even for a moment. Being around him made it hard to focus. Knowing that I planned to kill his uncle, a man Atticus cared for, wasn't an easy pill to swallow. Knowing just how sick Bexley was made it that much harder.

But I couldn't let my conscience get in the way.

A banging sounded on the other side of the wall, followed by a rather unladylike grunt. A moment later, the girl waddled back in with a large golden frame.

"Dad brought this home from Room the other day. I guess he'd had Melissa's son Harry paint this back before he died. When he gave it to Mom yesterday, it didn't go over so well. I'd never heard her swear so much."

Atticus removed the hand from his face. "Your mom swore?"

"Sure did." Bexley balanced the heavy frame on her foot. "I thought the neighbors were going to call the sheriff on them. Never seen Mom so mad."

Atticus stared at the back side of the painting. The artist signed and dated it only a few months ago.

"What's this got to do with Ember?"

"You're not going to believe it. It's like looking in a mirror, if that mirror turned back time, I mean." She shifted the frame onto one corner so she could slip her foot out. Then she rocked it from side to side. Leaning it against the desk, she paused to make sure it wasn't going to topple over and then stepped back.

"What the—" Atticus leaped up from his chair.

Bexley was right. It was like looking in a mirror. I rose from the settee to study the painting. The artist had a skilled eye. He'd captured my features with perfect strokes, including the blistering skin around my eye.

Words tried to form as they fell from Atticus's lips, but I ignored him.

"It's you, isn't it?" Bexley whispered. "Sorry, but your scars are kinda intense."

"Yes." I stared at the young girl who stood in the center of a blazing inferno. She wore a white nightgown, her hair draped in two braids. My gaze fell over the floral wallpaper behind the flames. This painting depicted roses instead of lilies, but it was close enough to reality. My gaze fell to the right-hand corner of the painting, and a sob caught in my throat.

"Momma." I collapsed to the ground and ran my fingertip over the image of the fallen woman. Her face was turned from sight, lost behind the wall of flames, but I knew it was her.

"That man." Atticus's words broke through my pain. I looked up to see him pointing. "Bexley, who is that?"

"Heck if I know. Looks a bit like dad, though." She squinted and then frowned. "Wow. It really looks like him. That's weird. I didn't think Harry knew Dad all that well. Maybe it's a coincidence? Trying to personalize his art for a paying client?"

"No." Atticus turned to look down at me. "That's no coincidence."

When his hand fell on my shoulder, I reacted without thinking. Atticus screamed as I twisted his hand. It took every ounce of willpower I possessed to hold back the burning in my hands.

"I'm sorry." His whisper tore through the waves of rage radiating through me at the sight of the painting. I tried to remember that I didn't want to hurt him. But there was something inside of me that was screaming for vengeance. For pain and darkness and death.

"It was my fault she burned," I sobbed, staring at the fireballs depicted in the girl's hands. My shimmering tears splattered against the floor.

"Ember, let me—"

"No!" I yanked back on his wrist until there was a sickening pop. His eyes bulged, and a gargled cry of pain escaped.

"Dad!" Bexley shrieked and started for the door. I shot out my free hand and sent a flame in her direction. She dove to the side at the last second.

"Don't hurt her," Atticus grunted. He'd dropped to one knee, fighting against my hold. "She's innocent."

"Innocent?" I laughed, sounding a bit crazed. I could only imagine that I looked it as well. "She is his daughter, Atticus."

"Yes, a girl like you. Forced into a life she didn't ask for."

Heat spiraled around me as I glared down at him. Another tingle in my palms intensified the heat, and Atticus began to squirm.

"Hurt me if you have to, but leave her out of it."

A reddish tint tainted my vision. Flames licked at the edges of my sight. Rage swirled in my heart and sank heavily into my stomach. In the back of my mind, I could hear the screams of my momma as she burned alive. "Mehki took everything from me."

"And for good reason," a voice said from behind me.

I whirled around, yanking Atticus with me as I turned to face the man I'd been hunting for years. He glanced to where his daughter cowered behind a chair. I spotted a woman backing away from the doorway over his shoulder. She was older, but shared Bexley's features.

"I knew you would come." He stepped into the room with a calm that unnerved me. "It was only a matter of time."

"Uncle?" Atticus grunted when I yanked on his arm again.

Mehki tsked and shook his head. "Leave it to you to fall for the enemy."

"She's not my enemy," he ground out. My hold on his hand eased as his words worked to help me see reason again.

"This girl killed your parents, Atticus. Orlon was at least smart enough to see the truth."

Atticus's eyes narrowed. "You're the one who told him about Ember?"

"Of course." He circled around me, keeping a fair distance between us, and then sat on the edge of his desk. His casual demeanor didn't fool me. I knew he'd chosen that spot for a reason. He most likely had a weapon hidden there. "I'd hoped he would rough her up enough so that he could bring her to me. Seems someone else decided to rescue her instead."

Realization began to dawn on Atticus. I watched the lines around his eyes soften. When he looked up at me, regret spilled in to take the place of his anger.

"Don't apologize," I said through gritted teeth. "You saved my life."

He nodded and remained silent. Mehki's laugh grated on my nerves as I turned to face him again. "Why?"

"That is the ultimate question, is it not?" He folded his hands in his lap. Black leather gloves covered them. I realized he was dressed. As if he'd been planning for this moment long before Atticus brought me to his doorstep.

"I'm sure you have a lot of questions. Most of which I don't care to answer. Your mom was in the wrong place at the wrong time. I never wanted her. Not after I found out you were adopted. I'm sure you already guessed that by now, since she never had your abilities. But you . . ." His smile made the hairs on the back of my neck stand up. "You were the ultimate prize. I have traced your lineage through the ages, followed your many lives. It's all quite fascinating. I have yet to actually find your origins. I'd ask you, but then I suppose you don't actually know."

"So just because I was adopted, my momma was useless to you?"

Mehki shrugged. "Yes."

My nails dug deep into my palms as I fought to hold back my rage.

"You son of a—"

Bexley peeked out from behind the chair. At his admission, she rose. "You killed her mom?"

"Bex, darling, sometimes sacrifices are made for the greater good." He held out his hand to his daughter. "I did it for you."

She stopped short of his hand. "For me?"

"Of course," a new voice joined the group. I turned to see that Mehki's wife no longer cowered in the dark. She stood in the doorway, her silver hair shining in the light. Her coffee-colored eyes were large behind the glasses perched on her nose. She looked frail and gaunt in the nightgown that hung loosely over her slight frame. "Ever since you were diagnosed as a child, Mehki has been obsessed with phoenix lore."

"What's wrong with her?" I asked Atticus and released my hold on him.

"She has a rare sickle cell disease." He rubbed his hands together. "The human doctors don't have a cure for it yet. Even Jared Lewis gave it a shot and failed. He has the ability to fix any disease, but it's almost like her body rejects any form of healing. We suspect that since she developed the disease at such a young age, her human side left her in a weakened state. Now it's preventing her shifter abilities from awakening."

"So Bexley is dying," I finished for him. "And you figured I could cure her."

"We were desperate." Atticus's aunt stepped into the room. "I couldn't lose my baby girl. Not when there was one last chance to hope."

Flames shot out from my palms and lit the fringe of the rug. Atticus hurried to stamp them out, wincing at the pain in the soles of his bare feet.

"Elora," Mehki called to his wife. "We don't have to explain ourselves. Our reasons are our own."

I took a step forward, but Atticus grabbed my arm and held me back. With the flicker of his gaze, I turned to see Mehki had a shotgun in his hands now.

"I realize you're blessed with immortality and this gun can't do a whole lot against you, but it sure can hurt." He set it on his lap. "I taught Orlon how to shoot, knowing one day that skill might come in handy. He almost succeeded with you. But I won't need this gun, because you're going to give me what I want without a fuss."

I snorted. "There's nothing you can do to make me."

"Oh, I reckon I'll be able to change your mind. You care for my nephew. It's easy to see. And I have something that's very dear to him." Mehki's smile stretched so wide, it became plastic. "I have his parents."

CHAPTER 14

For the span of a breath, the room fell into shocked silence. But just as quickly, it erupted into shouting.

"What do you mean, you have my parents?" Atticus raged. "Who did we bury?"

"I thought a phoenix killed Uncle Ridge and Aunt Jaelyn," Bexley said.

"You faked your own brother's death?" Elora gasped.

I remained silent, watching Mehki. He did the same with me. No one else in the room mattered to him. Not his dying daughter, grieving nephew, or distraught wife. And in that moment of clarity, I knew his entire family had been duped by a master manipulator.

"He wants me for himself," I said.

Atticus turned to look at me. "What?"

"This was never about healing Bexley or using your parents as a cover-up. He wants me. Wants what I can give him, isn't that right?"

Mehki's smile was cold. "Survivors do what they must, Ember?"

"Is she telling the truth?" Elora turned on her husband. "None of this was about healing Bexley?"

His silence was answer enough. So was the crazed look in his eye.

"It wouldn't have mattered," I said to his wife. "I can't heal others. Only myself."

A sob escaped Elora as she collapsed to the floor. Bexley rushed toward her mom and wrapped the shaking woman in her arms.

"It's okay," the teenager soothed, but the tears falling from her eyes told a different story.

"And my parents?" Atticus said, lifting his gaze from the women of his family. "They're alive?"

"Ridge may be a thorn in my side, but he's still blood." Mehki waved his hand as if the matter was trivial. "He still has his uses."

"You destroyed Orlon—made him feel like this was his fault—and for what?" Atticus threw out his hand toward me. "So you could kidnap her? What good does that do you if she can't heal anyone else?"

Mehki surged to his feet. "You always were too short-sighted to see the bigger picture. That girl isn't a walking doctor. She's a gift. Her tears contain the secret to immortality. If we can collect enough of her essence, then I can live forever."

Elora sniffed. "How could you do this to us? To your only daughter?"

"Immortality is everything, my dear. Once I discover its secrets, I can save you and Bex."

"And my parents?" Atticus pressed. He shifted his stance. When he did so, I realized he was maneuvering his way between me and his uncle.

"Yes, they can live, too," Mehki said in a flippant tone. "Under my rule, of course. Ridge doesn't deserve to lead our family. The Roc Aerie needs a strong leader."

"He was strong before you murdered him." Atticus took another step.

I grabbed hold of Atticus's arm, and he looked back at me. "So you are a roc."

"We changed our name to Laroc ages ago, but that's our species." He looked confused for a split second before realization dawned on him. "Ember, it's not what you think. I would never . . . I didn't . . ."

"But you already have betrayed her, Atticus. It's in your blood, that thirst for hers." Mehki laughed. "You know well enough that we're the only known mortal enemy of a phoenix. The only being capable of killing her. The guns just make the process a little more fun."

Atticus stiffened and looked back at me. "I'm not like him."

"Of course you aren't, boy. At least not enough to finish the job for me. But Orlon is." When Mehki looked over my shoulder, I turned to see Atticus's brother standing in the doorway.

"Oh, crap." I took the brunt of his tackle hard to the chest. My head slammed into the hardwood floor, and the room started to grow dark as his hands found my neck again.

"Get off her!" Atticus appeared over me, yanking against his brother, but Orlon was crazed. The maniacal look in his eye told me that I had no choice but to fight back.

"Atticus," I coughed, fighting to speak. "Run!"

The instant Atticus's hands slipped from his brother's shoulder, I slammed my hands into Orlon's chest. The man erupted into flames. His screams rose into shrieks. Bexley cried out when Orlon shot to his feet, flapping his arms as they shifted into wings. By the time he hit the large window and took flight, the flames had engulfed him.

"Orlon!" Atticus screamed into the night, hanging out the window in search of his brother.

I coughed and rolled to my side. Elora sat staring at me with horror. She ignored Bexley's pleading to run.

A violent tug on my hair sent me flying up into the air. I found my footing just before Mehki dragged me from the room. I twisted and fought back, but he remained out of reach of each flame that I threw at him.

The wallpaper in the foyer caught fire. The drapes began to smoke. I carved deep scorch marks into the floors.

"Ember!" Atticus appeared in the doorway.

"Atticus, no!" But my cry of warning was too late.

Mehki turned on his nephew as Atticus leaped. His hand shifted into talons and raked across his nephew's chest. I watched as Atticus's shirt and flesh split, spilling blood onto the floor. When he fell, he didn't move.

"No!" I reached back and took hold of Mehki's hand. The scent of his bubbling flesh burned my eyes.

A hard backhand with his claw sent my head spinning as I collapsed to the ground. Lifting me as if I weighed no more than a bag of feathers, he slammed me repeatedly into the wall. Shimmering gold and crimson tears fell from my eyes as my nose cracked and the skin over my temple split.

Something smooth and cold touched my cheek. Fighting against my swelling eye, I spied the small glass vial he used to capture my essence. His grin made my blood boil.

"Get off me." Heat burst from my hands, and Mehki flew backward. He hit high on the wall, shattering a mirror, and then fell to the floor.

I dragged myself over to where Atticus lay in a pool of blood. His chest was sliced open, the torn skin flapping when I rolled him over.

"You have to shift." I took hold of his hand. "It's the only way to heal."

He groaned as he nodded. I watched as his right arm flopped against the ground, trying to extend into a wing. A few feathers sprouted and then nothing.

"I can't." When he wheezed, his words sounded wet from the blood filling his lungs.

"Don't you die on me," I pleaded. Tearing my tank top over my head, I pressed it to his wounds. Mere seconds was all it took to soak through. There would be no stopping the bleed out. His wounds were too severe.

"I'm . . ." He gasped as bubbles of blood burst at his lips. "I'm so sorry."

"Shh." I pressed his hand to my face. "It's okay. I understand."

"No." He tried to roll to his side, but the effort was too much. "I know you. You're . . . a . . . good . . ."

"Atticus!" I shook his shoulders when his eyes fell closed. "No. You can't leave me!"

I pressed my cheek to his chest. The blood didn't matter. Only the fading sound of his beating heart did. My tears fell as I felt his life draining away.

"He can't save you now, girl."

I screamed as Mehki's hand latched around my calf and dragged me away from Atticus. I twisted and fought, kicking and screaming, but he didn't relent. He was in mid-shift, and his strength far outweighed my own.

His feathers were far darker than Atticus's, black and etched with the silver of his hair. His talons were razor sharp as they tore into my leg and shredded muscle. His beak had a wicked curve to it, sharp enough to tear flesh from my bones as he tossed me out the front door.

By the time he reached his porch, he was full roc. If I had thought Atticus was big, he was nothing compared to Mehki.

"How can you kill your own family?" I screamed at him. The hole that had opened in my heart grew with each passing second. The only relief I could find was that Atticus's suffering was over. But it killed me to not be there with him in the final moments.

Mehki twisted his head around but didn't answer. I didn't know if he even could. Fluffy had been able to speak when he was in his wolf form. I suspected that even if Mehki could speak around his beak, he would choose not to.

I screamed as he grabbed me in one talon and took to the air. This flight was nothing like what I'd experienced with Atticus. The beating of his wings stole the air from my lungs as we shot high into the air. I feared my neck would snap from the force.

My ability to wield fire was useless in the face of certain death from a fall at this height. So instead of fighting, I held on for dear life. With each flap of his wings, my stomach dropped and spun. Nausea gripped me as I closed my eyes, but the instant I did so, I realized that made it worse.

When a terrible cry echoed around me, I clasped my hands over my ears and yelled. The cry filled the air, permeating every inch of space around me and in me. It was only after something huge slammed into us that I realized the cry hadn't come from Mehki.

"Atticus!" I stared in disbelief at the white-streaked bird that clung to Mehki, digging his claws in. Streaks of blood lined his feathered breast, but when he looked at me, I saw life in his eyes. "But how?"

Anchoring himself on his uncle's back, he lifted one wing. I stared in disbelief at the golden shimmer of my tears threading through his feathers. I laughed through my tears. "I healed you."

I didn't know how it could be possible. My tears hadn't worked as I clung to my momma's smoldering body. Or kissed Susan's cheek while she lay recovering from a heart attack in the hospital a year ago. But why didn't matter. He was alive.

Mehki's talon loosened its grip when Atticus raked his claws across the length of his back. I screamed as I fell, tumbling end over end. Screeching erupted in the air. The rushing of wind soon drowned it out.

I'm going to die. Again.

"Umph," I groaned when I landed hard on the back of a bird. This one had chestnut markings with a brilliant white head. The side of the bird was black and scarred.

"You're alive!" The instant relief rushed in, I remembered why I'd had to burn Orlon in the first place.

Orlon dove straight to the ground, pulling up at the very last second. I saw my dinner for the second time as he skidded to a stop and ruffled his feathers, sending me rolling to the ground.

"Why is my brother attacking Mehki? Is it because of you?" His human hand wrapped around my throat within seconds of landing. I could see the extent of his burns. His skin peeled back to reveal raw flesh. "Answer me!"

I pried at his fingers, gasping for air. He seemed to take a hint and relaxed his grip enough for me to be able to speak.

"Mehki lied." I sucked in another breath. "Parents . . . alive."

"What?" He yanked me so hard, I worried my hip would shake right out of its socket. "Explain."

"Killed . . . my momma. Faked your parents' deaths. Still . . . alive."

His eyes flashed a dark gold, then he turned to stare at his brother's desperate attack on Mehki. "If you are lying, I will shred you where you stand."

"If I'm not . . . Atticus will die . . . while you stand here . . . threatening me," I ground out.

With a disgusted snarl, he tossed me away. He shifted and shot up into the sky. I rolled onto my back to watch him join the fight.

Great droplets of blood fell from the sky. It was impossible to tell who was winning. The three birds spiraled in a ball of feathers and claws. Their cries echoed off the mountains.

Struggling to my feet, I hurried to wipe my damp cheeks, spreading my healing tears on the worst of the wounds in my leg. Spreading the second dose on my eye, I regained vision in that eye. The healing warmth spread through my body.

Taking in my surroundings, I realized that Orlon had dropped me off on the slope leading to Atticus's cabin. The climb was steep and arduous as the ground gave way beneath me. I fought to climb as I tried to keep an eye on the fight in the sky.

A teeth-rattling shriek nearly sent me rolling to the bottom. I searched the skies and spotted a dark figure plummeting to the ground. Trees cracked, and a great cloud of dirt rushed into the air where it landed.

Desperate to know who it was, I wrapped my hand around a tree and leaned out over the ravine. Circling in the sky were the two remaining birds. One black. One light.

"He's still alive." Sweet relief swept in as I hugged the tree. "Come on, Atticus. Make him pay!"

The final hundred feet of the climb left me panting on the ground at the top. Dust clung to my bloody legs.

From behind me, the roof of Atticus's cabin exploded. Splinters of wood sliced my skin as I covered my head. The walls groaned but held firm. The windows shattered under the impact of the birds suddenly plummeting from the sky.

Peering through the dust cloud, I stared at the front door. "Come on, Atticus."

I leaped to my feet when I heard a shrill scream followed by a sickening crunch. "No!"

Racing toward the cabin, I skidded to a stop at the driveway when the door opened, and Mehki stepped out. Scratches, torn strips of muscle, and blood clothed his nakedness. So much blood.

"Atticus!" I screamed.

Mehki's gaze shifted to meet mine. When he did, he smiled. It was the same smile he wore when he stepped over my momma's body. Triumph.

"You bastard!"

The phoenix tattoo on my forearm spread its wings, and a scorching heat spread along my body. Tongues of fire danced over my skin. The fibers of Atticus's Led Zeppelin shirt shriveled and became ash. The light radiating from me pulsated. My vision darkened despite the intensity of the light. Like a roaring wind, I felt the power surge through me and then burst free.

Mehki raised a hand to shield himself. I screamed at the jolt of released power, and my vision exploded into flame.

CHAPTER 15

*T*he world around me burned. A vibrant orange glow lit the expanse of the night sky and forced the stars into hiding. The temperate air made the oxygen feel thin in my lungs. I rolled to my side and brushed singed leaves from my naked body. With each labored exhale, the rain of ash drifted like feathers on a gentle breeze and then spiraled away.

I coughed and took a quick inventory of my condition. The throbbing in my head made my thoughts hazy. Weariness weighed on me as I sat up. Nothing within my body appeared to be broken.

There was no sound apart from the crackling of fire all around. No wolf's cry to the moon or the hoot of an owl swooping overhead. The sudden absence of insect song was eerie.

"Atticus?"

My voice resonated in my chest, sounding both unnatural and louder than I'd expected. The call trailed off when I saw that I was surrounded by some sort of a shimmering gold force field. It was visible only from the corner of my eye. The hairs on my arms rose. My fingertips tingled as I traced the ground in search of an end to this mysterious force. I discovered that it arched over my head, completely surrounding me.

"Whoa," I whispered, in awe of the raw power emanating from the barrier. "Well, that's new."

My hair floated off my shoulders, drawn to the current of electricity when I tried to push against the barrier. The few stray hairs caught my eye, and I gasped. Each strand had shifted to onyx.

"At least black is my color." I coughed.

When I moved to brush my hair back, I stopped. Where my fingers brushed against my face, smooth skin lay instead of scar tissue. I traced the edge of my eye and around my lip, but there were no ridges from my burns.

"Oh, my god," I wept as I explored my new and perfect face. "I'm healed."

But with this new joy came a profound sense of emptiness.

"Atticus? Please tell me you're still alive in there." I waved my arm to try to clear away some of the ash falling from overhead so that I could see the cabin. I realized with a start that none of it touched me. It was blocked by the shield surrounding me.

That's when I noticed the obvious shaking of my hands. Not from shock, though that would be justifiable at the moment, but from power. It was unlike anything I'd felt before. It rippled through me like an electrical current, charged and ready for use at a second's notice.

I clenched my hands. The sensations were too much. I needed answers, someone to explain what happened, but I was alone. An inferno raged all around me. Lifeless trees were uprooted and tossed thirty feet away. Those that remained were nothing more than burnt stumps. The grass was blistered. This part of the mountain was a landslide of devastation.

My knees were weak at the sight of it when I stood. As I turned in a full circle, I knew that I was standing in the epicenter of something truly terrible. A suffocating sadness dragged at me at the thought of so much loss. The animals that survived wouldn't have a home to return to. The forest would take years to regrow.

As I moved toward the scorched cabin and stepped over a pile of charred bone dust, I knew why Mehki was gone. There was no one left alive. No one apart from me.

I looked down at my naked form. I was completely unsoiled by the flames. My skin was washed clean of the blood and healed of all wounds. It was almost as if I'd become a new person.

My breath caught. "Like I was reborn from the fire."

Twisting my arm to look at my phoenix tattoo, I saw a small baby bird lying in a pile of embers. It fluttered its wings and then nestled down to sleep.

"From the embers a new phoenix will rise," I whispered, repeating the phrase I'd read during my search into the lore. "Atticus was right. I am a phoenix."

Though my transformation didn't come in the way the lore spoke of, I knew I'd found my kind.

Maybe sometimes legends and myth get things wrong. I hoped so, because that might mean there was someone else like me out there. Someone who could help me understand who I was.

My fingers began to tremble as I closed my eyes so that the shimmering of the force field was hidden from sight. I breathed in what felt like my first real breath of air. I knew what I was finally. And no matter how scary that might be, it was right.

"If only Atticus could have seen this transformation," I whispered. My eyes shot open. "The cabin!"

The thought of his final moments sent me racing toward the charred steps. They crumbled underfoot, but I didn't fall. My force field held me up.

"Please be alive." I kicked aside the smoldering remains of the door and clambered over the fallen timbers.

I stopped short when I caught sight of a burnt corpse. It was kneeling on the floor, its hands raised against the wall of flame that had consumed him.

"No!"

I collapsed at Atticus's side. The feeling of loss was too great. Though his facial features were unrecognizable, I knew it was him. My heart couldn't deny the truth of it, and my eyes would never be able to erase this horrible scene.

"You can't leave me," I begged, reaching out for him. My fingers hung in the air less than an inch from his face. "You were right about me. I need to believe that there's good in me, but there's something more now. Something dark and angry. I need you to show me how to come back from this!"

I hung my head, unable to look at his scorched form any longer, while violent sobs racked my body. I did this. I killed the only man that I'd ever let myself care about.

Wrenching back my head, I released a soul-shattering scream into the night. It overshadowed the crackling of the fire and the splintering of trees. My fists beat against the wood floor that he'd built with his own hands. With each hit, a surge of shimmering gold raced across the floor. The wooden boards split and groaned. The cabin began to lean.

"No!" I lunged forward to try to catch Atticus.

His form began to crumble in a slow tide. His nose dissolved first. Then his cheeks and forehead. His right arm fell away, followed by part of his left side. As I tried to hold him together, his embers slipped through my quaking fingers, nothing left but a pile of ash.

In that moment, I forgot how to breathe. The numbness that I felt wasn't a complete lack of feeling. Instead, it was a volatile overload of so many emotions that I couldn't process them all at once.

Atticus was dead. Because of me.

The swirl of my emotions funneled into suffocating despair. My heart splintered into a thousand pieces. My hands glowed a brilliant red. My hair sparked with electricity as my vision exploded in an array of color.

Stretching out my arms, I felt a dark power pulsating through and around me. I became one with the dying trees. The frantic heartbeats of the animals fleeing my destruction echoed in my ears. Then I became aware of the screams from the valley below.

An invisible force lifted me into the air through the hole in the cabin's roof, and I glimpsed the extent of the damage for the first time. Half of the mountain was obliterated. Cars were overturned on countless streets, their wheels spinning and on fire. The ski lift was decimated and the lodge engulfed in flames. I saw several figures fleeing from their ruins, their clothes alight.

The firestorm I'd unleashed had made its way to Havenwood Falls. The roads leading into town oozed tar. The high school was trapped by the landslide, buried by several feet of molten earth. The main street was lit with an unquenchable blaze as the shops burned.

The roof of the motorcycle club had collapsed. The clock tower of City Hall was a rising pyre into the night. I glanced down at the burning remains of Broastful Brew and a sob caught in my throat. What if Mabel was still in there? Smoke billowed out of the shattered windows, but I couldn't see any movement.

Beside it, the dove-gray awning of Melissa's art shop was scorched. Tears streamed down my cheeks when I saw her sitting on the street, huddled over a wailing child in her arms. Her blond hair was matted with soot.

The gazebo where I'd watched the play was demolished into splinters, the fountain charred black. The painted front of Shear Magic where I'd been offered a free wax was blistered. I rose higher and saw several bodies with smoke rising from their torsos outside of Coffee Haven.

"What have I done?" My voice quaked as numbness raced through me like a cold rain.

Dozens of screams rose from the apartments by the ski resort. I could see people waving pillow cases out the windows, desperate to be saved before the fires reached them. Several people stood in shock outside Whisper Falls Inn.

Everywhere I looked, I saw pain, fear, and desolation. It hit me like a wrecking ball to my gut, and I closed my eyes as my stomach heaved.

As countless alarms blared, creatures of all sorts took to the air and streets to fight back the fires. Humans sat in front of smoldering homes, mourning the loss of their loved ones. I wondered if the little girl I'd bought a balloon for was among the children I'd killed tonight.

Those supernaturals who had survived worked their way through the town giving aid. The community, both human and nonhuman, came together. Their sheer love for one another made me want to hurtle myself out of the sky so I could be rid of my guilt.

How could I have allowed my grief to bring me to this point? To harm so many innocent people?

My grief battled with a new sensation, one that reveled in this death. Voices filled my mind, sinister in their whispers. They weren't done with me.

"No." I closed my eyes to the pain. "This isn't me. These people didn't deserve this. Atticus cared for them, and for good reason. They are decent, loving people."

At least they were before I arrived.

"What about Bexley and Elora?" I whispered, turning to see if I could spy their house, but it was too hard to see through the smoke. I still had no clue if Orlon had survived the fall. If he didn't get out of the woods in time, I sealed his fate for him.

I searched for Sheriff Kasun's vehicle but couldn't find it. But there, near the fire department, I spotted the shine of Lloyd's badge. He was trapped halfway under a mangled car. The skin on his face was melted.

"No," I sobbed, wrapping my arms around myself. "This can't be happening."

Rising high enough to see the waters of the falls boiling, I peered into its distorted reflection. I saw myself, a naked girl surrounded by the fiery image of a magnificent flaming bird. Though I couldn't say for sure at this height, I would've sworn that my eyes glowed red.

Currents of power swirled around my hands, fighting to be unleashed. This new rage thirsted for blood, for revenge. But as I looked at the cabin, I saw the pile of ash where Mehki once stood. He was finally dead. I got what I'd wanted for so many years.

But looking out over the valley, I knew the cost of my revenge was far too great.

I threw out my hands and stopped rising in the air. "This can't be. I won't allow it."

My body hummed with energy as I began to spin. I didn't know what I was doing, only that I had to do something. A golden vortex appeared beneath me as I focused my powers inward. It tore at the ground, ripping aged trees up by their roots and spitting them out as the funnel whipped around.

My bones rattled and my stomach lurched as I pushed myself faster. The light around me grew so intense that it was almost as if I'd become the blazing inferno of the sun. The heat blistered as if I had landed on the star's very surface, and in that split second, my inner being burst apart.

Then everything stopped.

I hung, suspended in air. It was neither warm nor cold. It felt like nothing at all, and on the same hand, it was everything. Every beating heart, every laugh and child's cry. It was every kiss shared between lovers and tear shed for those that'd died.

This place was an infinite stream of time. Shards of light floated around me. Each one glistened with colors no human eye had ever glimpsed before. There was no sound of the vortex or the screaming of the dying. Time stood still as I reached out to touch the nearest shard. It glittered with power. With life.

"It's beautiful." My voice echoed around me without end.

The shards jingled like a glass wind chime as they floated into each other. It was peaceful here. Then just as quickly as I entered this strange place, time and my life force ricocheted back into my body. I was flung from the sky. Like a falling meteor, I fell in a blaze of flame. A crater formed when I hit, and darkness consumed me.

∾

WHEN I OPENED MY EYES, I swayed in place, blinded by the light that emanated from me. Mehki stood less than five feet from the cabin steps, his hands raised to ward off the light. Through the glass door, I saw Atticus was shifting back into a man.

"He's not dead!" I gasped. A tear fell. Then another.

I've been here before. The sensation of déjà vu was too strong to ignore as I blinked and tried to remember. Something terrible was about to happen. But what?

When Mehki took a step toward me, I knew that I could kill him. I raised my hand, intending to take revenge for what he'd stolen from me, but I stopped. My fingers refused to open, though I was desperate to release this newfound power. Strands of onyx hair tangled in my eyelashes. The transformation had begun.

"I remember this." My voice echoed and bounced back at me. That's when I saw the force field beginning to form, and panic sent me into action. "Not again!"

I yanked my hand back. Pressing my palm against my chest, I focused the full brunt of the firestorm on myself. Mehki's cry of alarm faded as the light exploded and I flew back into the woods. Trees cracked and fell with each impact. The force field shimmered but remained intact as my world exploded into flame. The fires ate at my skin, melting it away until I was sure nothing more than bone remained.

Never before had I experienced such pain. It stole my breath away as thousands of tongues of flames licked across my body. Gold and crimson shimmered around me, and then with a brilliant burst of blue, it vanished.

I don't know how much time passed as I lay trapped in torment. It felt like days before I deciphered a shout.

"Ember!"

I couldn't move when Atticus's arms wrapped around me and cradled me against his chest. His skin was sticky, matted with blood and feathers. My head lolled to the side. Before the darkness swept in for the second time, I realized that I was lucky to still have a body for him to pick up.

EPILOGUE

 hen I awoke, I wasn't surprised to find myself tied to a hospital bed. Or to see a rather grim looking sheriff staring back at me. What did surprise me was to find a few other familiar faces at the end of my bed.

Bexley stood hugging her mom, Elora. I wasn't sure which one was holding the other one up. Orlon leaned on a crutch. His right arm was tucked into a sling and his left leg trapped in a cast that went almost to his groin. Bloody gauze was wrapped around his head, covering a bump. But he had a wry smile on his face when he noticed that I was awake.

"Looks like Sleeping Beauty finally decided to join the party after all." He chuckled. Then he winced when Bexley jabbed him with an elbow in his side.

"How do you feel, Ember?"

I turned to see Atticus sitting right where Susan should be. His face was more black and blue than skin-toned. His arm was in a matching sling to Orlon's, but the smile on his face was perfect.

"You're alive!" I shot up in bed, but the restraints stopped me.

Sheriff Kasun smirked. "You won't be sneaking out of this hospital any time soon."

"Want to bet?" Atticus and I said at the same time. I laughed and felt a sharp pain in my ribs. Apparently, I still had a bit of healing to finish.

Atticus eased me back. "The doctors said you should be dead. Turns out you had other plans."

I smiled. "I could say the same for you."

His brow dipped in confusion. "Yeah, about that. You kept mumbling that I was dead while you were sleeping. Planning on finishing the job later or something?"

I looked at each of the people standing around my bedside. "You don't know?"

"Know what?" Sheriff Kasun stepped forward.

"The town . . . the fire . . ." I shook my head. "I killed everyone."

Atticus and the sheriff exchanged a long glance before Ric snorted and shook his head. "If that's not the ramblings of a concussion—"

"No, it's not—" I stopped when Atticus squeezed my hand. "Sure. Yeah. That must be it."

Ric Kasun's eyes narrowed at me, but then he shrugged and headed for the door. "Tate is on watch, in case you try to make an escape. I've given him orders to bite on sight. What with you being immortal and all, we figure it'd just be a flesh wound."

"Good to know." From around the corner, the younger officer flashed me a grin.

"We should get Orlon home to rest," Elora said. She patted the blanket over my foot and pulled Bexley along. "I'm glad you're alive, Ember. If I had known—"

"You didn't," I said. I gave her a nod. A small but awkward smile lit her face before she nodded back. We had an understanding. Mehki had hidden the monster well, but all evil gets found out eventually.

"Hey!" I called, and Elora turned back. "When I get out of here, I'd like to try something with Bex. I might be able to help your daughter."

Her eyes widened, and she looked to Atticus, who smiled in return. "I told you she was something special."

Elora smiled and nodded. "Any help you could give would be very much appreciated."

She didn't need to apologize for Mehki's actions. It wasn't her place to do so.

Deep down, I knew the price I'd almost paid for my revenge. A mother's love ran deeper than even that. I couldn't fault her for wanting her daughter to live. I'd have probably done the same thing if given the chance to bring my momma back.

"Rest up, little firebird. When you're feeling better, we'll teach you how to fly." Orlon smiled.

"Seriously?" I blinked. "I can do that?"

Atticus laughed. "After what I saw in the woods last night, I doubt there's much you can't do."

"Wait!" I called as Orlon turned to leave. "What about your parents? Mehki said they were still alive."

A shadow fell over his face. "Yeah. Well, Mehki's not doing much talking now that he's been turned over to the Court, but word will spread. People will help us look. We'll find them."

"Count me in on that search party. I'm pretty good at tracking," I said. He shot a pointed glance at my restraints, and I laughed. "Well, when I'm free, that is."

"I'll take it. And thanks for not letting me kill you. I'd have felt pretty bad about that after this came to light." Orlon waved his good hand and then hobbled out into the hallway.

"I told you he's not a half-bad guy when he's not trying to kill you." Atticus leaned over and rewarded me with that lopsided grin I'd come to love so much.

"Yeah. Funny how that changes a person." I leaned my forehead against his chin and breathed him in. I didn't think I'd ever find another scent that I liked more. "You going to tell me what happened after I passed out?"

"Not much to tell. Ric showed up with the cavalry right after you went all flame ball. I guess a three-bird brawl in the sky caught a few people's attention, and the Court had to do some cleanup work. They sent Ric to investigate. I was just getting my feet under me again when I saw Mehki make a run for it. I yelled out to Ric that Mehki faked my parents' deaths, and that was all it took. Personally, I think Ric enjoyed taking my uncle down. He wasn't the most popular man around town, if you hadn't guessed."

I smiled. "And you don't remember a firestorm or dying?"

Atticus's frown returned. I hated to steal away his smile again, but I needed to know. "It's time that you tell me what really happened out there, Ember."

I relayed to him as much as I could remember. It wasn't much more than the feeling of total desolation followed by peace. I couldn't have explained how I altered time if I wanted to. And then came the flames. Those I remembered.

"My face!" I yanked my arm up to try to check for my scars, but the bindings held tight.

"Easy." Atticus reached behind him and then lifted a mirror for me to see. "Look."

I couldn't believe my eyes. I was beautiful. Perfect and whole, the way I'd been after the firestorm. "I don't understand. I fixed everything back to the way it was."

Atticus set aside the mirror and took my hand in his. "When I found you lying in the woods, you looked like an angel, all glowing and shimmering. I was almost afraid to touch you, but I couldn't help myself. That's when I saw your scars were healing. And there was something else . . ."

"What?" I twined my fingers through his.

"You were calling my name."

"I was?" A blush rose to my cheeks, and I started to look away, but he stopped me.

"It meant the world to me," he whispered. But then he gave me his lopsided grin. "And don't you go thinking that you look any better than you did yesterday. I never saw those scars, remember? You've always taken my breath away."

The tenderness in his gaze as he brushed his fingers across my newly healed skin made my heart swell with love.

"Wow," I whispered.

"What?"

"I just realized that I kinda like you." I grinned.

"It's about time you figured that out." He smirked. "My being the only one able to see your tattoo come to life should have been your first hint. Guess you're a bit slow on the uptake."

"Oh, you—"

Atticus crushed his lips against mine. The fluttering of wings on my forearm told me that my tattoo was preening. I almost laughed, knowing he was right, but this kiss was too good to ruin.

I didn't know what would happen to Mehki or how the Court would make him pay for his crimes. I only hoped that I'd be around to see it. In the coming days, I knew that I'd have to account for my own actions. Sheriff Kasun seemed like a decent guy, and I vowed that I would pay my time, however long that was. After that, I figured I'd stick around Havenwood Falls for a while.

Atticus would wait for me. I knew that. Just like I knew that I'd need to speak to Addie about adding some extra warding to my tattoo. Something that would help prevent me from ever setting off another firestorm again.

But that could wait. This kiss, this moment with Atticus, was all that mattered. And for the first time in my life, I felt whole.

We hope you enjoyed this story in the Havenwood Falls series featuring a variety of supernatural creatures. The series is a collaborative effort by multiple authors.

Books in the main Havenwood Falls series:

Forget You Not by Kristie Cook
Old Wounds by Susan Burdorf
Fate, Love & Loyalty by E.J. Fechenda
Covetousness by Randi Cooley Wilson
The Winged & the Wicked by T.V. Hahn & Kristie Cook
Alpha's Queen by Lila Felix
Ink & Fire by R.K. Ryals
Lose You Not by Kristie Cook
Tragic Ink by Heather Hildenbrand
Nowhere to Hide by Belinda Boring
Flames Among the Frost by Amy Hale
Rock Me Gently by Susan Burdorf
From the Embers by Amy Miles
Defying Gravity by Kallie Ross
Gypsy Heart by Randi Cooley Wilson (August 2018)
Break Me Not by Kristie Cook (September 2018)

More books releasing on a monthly basis

Also try the YA line, Havenwood Falls High, and the historical paranormal line, Legends of Havenwood Falls

Stay up to date at www.HavenwoodFalls.com

Subscribe to our reader group and receive free stories and more!

ABOUT THE AUTHOR

Amy Miles is the author of multiple published novels, including her bestselling young adult immortals books, The Arotas Series. Unwilling to be defined by any one genre, she has written paranormal romance, science fiction/fantasy, post-apocalyptic, romance, inspirational, and plans to continue to explore new genres. She is the co-Founder of Red Coat PR, a firm helping indie authors build a marketing base for their career.

She is also the co-Founder of Penned Con, an annual two-day convention held in St. Louis, Missouri, bringing readers and authors together with industry professionals to learn, grow, and give back. She and her husband are heavily involved in charity work through Action for Autism, a St. Louis–based organization aiding families with autism, and founded the Penned Con scholarship to benefit area families. She is an avid reader, urban homesteader, weekend golfer, and Netflix binge addict who lives with her husband and son in South Carolina.

ACKNOWLEDGMENTS

For every book that I write, there is always a team of people working on the sidelines to support me.

I'm first and foremost grateful for my husband, Rick Miles, and son, Landon, for giving me the time and headspace that I need to get through another project. I know that when I'm in the writing cave I can be insanely focused, and it's hard to pull myself out of that to have family time. Heck, sleep and a shower seem optional some days. Far too many days I tend to get these mile-long stares into nothingness when I'm struggling with a particular section of a book, and they kindly leave me be until I have it sorted in my head. They are my rocks.

My endless thanks go out to Danielle Bannister, for not only being with me every step of the way through each of my books, while listening to me moan and whine and cry over frustrating plot lines or characters that refuse to behave, but also for being my chip gal. She is always there to tell me that any time is chip time. And believe me, that's a real life saver. She also beta read *From the Embers* before anyone else. The fact that she liked it was a HUGE win, since we are polar opposites. Your comments are invaluable to me, Danielle. I couldn't stay sane without you.

To my Badass Betas, words cannot express how you have helped me over the years. Just knowing that my book doesn't suck before it goes to edits gives me hope that when it's all polished and shiny, it will be worth reading. Thank you for taking this wild ride with me.

A huge thank you goes out to all of the Havenwood Falls authors. You guys are the best. Seeing all of your excitement over the project mingled with a bit of crazy that I know all too well is inspiring. Thank you for letting me be a part of this journey.

Thank you to Kristie Cook, Liz Ferry, and Regina Wamba for being the powerhouse team behind this project. You guys make us look good.

And lastly, I wouldn't be where I am today without amazing readers. You guys get my own personal weird, and I love you for it. Thank you for supporting Havenwood Falls and making it a blast.

~ A Havenwood Falls New Adult Novella ~

Havenwood Falls

Defying Gravity

Kallie Ross

AN EXCERPT

Defying Gravity (A Havenwood Falls Novella) by Kallie Ross

The weight of tradition grows heavier on Tate Kasun each day. As a wolf shifter, he knows the ancient magic of Havenwood Falls must be protected. As the son of the sheriff, he's expected to safeguard that magic from outsiders. But then Alex Newton crashes into Tate's world and makes him question whom and what he should be protecting.

After years of trying to prove the supernatural world doesn't exist, Alex Newton stumbles into Havenwood Falls, past their protective wards, and into the arms of Tate Kasun. Alex discovers that the ancient ring she wears holds the power to give life, while making her immune to the magic around her—which not only makes her a threat to the Court of the Sun and the Moon, but puts her in imminent danger from those who want the power for themselves.

Alex is pulled into a world she can't explain. Tate is drawn to Alex in a way he can't deny. Will Tate defy his pack and put Havenwood Falls at risk to protect Alex? Or will he be able to convince the town to trust his instincts and pull together to protect this outsider?

DEFYING GRAVITY

AN EXCERPT

Technically, summer was a week away, but it appeared the winter still had a hold in the shadows of the forest along Mount Alexa. I'd never experienced what I considered cold weather in June, since I'd never before traveled to Colorado. I explored beyond the trail, feeling comfortable on the mountain because we had something in common. Our names were the same, only I went by Alex.

My good sense of direction and constant attention to my compass should have had me at the ridge of the mountain in another hour. Navigating around the trees and patches of snow wasn't too difficult—I'd prepared and conditioned for the outdoors back in Arizona.

I hated to admit it, but my last breakup had inspired my trip. The guy hadn't been that bad. In no way was I running away. I'd just finally realized I was wasting away while waiting for him to commit, and so was my work.

I would be better off with a dog anyway.

Driving to Colorado had always been the goal, and I'd decided I wouldn't let a dead-end relationship get in the way of me getting my doctorate. It was time to see if what I had inside me could change the world, or at least *my* world.

Buds of green had begun to dot the bare, gray bark sprawled overhead. The branches fractured the last of the day's sunlight, and my chest burned from breathing in the brisk mountain air. All the locals in the last town I drove through wore shorts and tank tops like there was a heat wave, but growing up in the desert had me donning a jacket and jeans everywhere I went.

I had one month to finish my research, two months tops, then I'd be defending my dissertation. I didn't know what would come next, but it would definitely not include dating. I wanted to make sure the next guy I invested myself into was a best friend. Someone who would invest in me, and not only his own academic aspirations. Sitting in classrooms for six years, researching hundreds of case studies, and hiking through these "haunted" forests had all been in hopes of helping people like me.

Snap.

The sound of a twig breaking interrupted my train of thought, and I made a sharp turn to find the woodland creature who'd crossed my path. Nothing was there. The sound of crunching leaves underfoot brought me to a stop. My heart pounded in my chest, and I took in a deep breath.

A low purr drifted toward me, followed by an extra-large tawny mountain lion. He had golden eyes and black edges around his ears and at the end of his lowered tail.

"Shoo," I commanded in a panic. "Back off."

He raised his head and sniffed the air.

"You're a nice kitty, aren't you?" I rambled. "I'm Alex Newton, and you are? You look like a Mr. Kitty. You don't have to call me Ms. Newton. Alex is fine. Are you feeling peckish?"

The mountain lion's tongue curled over his top teeth as he prowled toward me. A gust of wind rustled the leaves above us and blew my dark curly hair into my eyes. After tucking the strands behind my ears, I peeled the straps of my pack off my shoulders and held the bag between me and the cat like a shield.

"Okay, you don't have to go if you don't want to, Mr. Kitty." My voice shook.

I began to back up, and moved my hands behind my back. My feet dragged along the ground in slow motion, not wanting to startle the big cat. A few feet behind me, my fingers brushed up against a tree. There was no place to run without having to dodge a giant tree trunk or pass a wild, hungry animal. I'd wandered into his trap.

"You can have my bag. There's some beef jerky and trail mix." I slid another few inches, bringing my back flush against the tree's rough bark. "It'll taste way better than me."

I did remember reading about mountain lion attacks, but the article focused on how non-confrontational the cats were. Maybe I could escape while he tried to figure out the tricky zipper.

I tossed my bag a few feet in front of me. Mr. Kitty approached the backpack and pushed at it with his paw. My keys jingled against each other inside. And that's when it dawned on me—my car keys would be the mountain lion's new cat toy.

It's what I deserved for wandering off the trail. I thought I remembered leaving one of the backseat doors unlocked. If only I could get inside the car, I knew I could out-wait the mountain lion.

Suddenly, the cat's ears flattened and a low growl vibrated in his chest. One of my thumbs hooked into my back pocket, where I'd been carrying a decent-sized pocket knife. I'd have to worry about getting my car started later.

"Whoa, big guy, I don't want to hurt you." My gold thumb ring glinted as I swung my knife in front of me and flicked a notch on the side of the gadget. The blade popped out. I doubted the knife would stop the mountain lion, but it could do some damage and maybe buy me some time.

With a glance at my surroundings, I still had nowhere to run. I'd have to distract the mountain lion somehow, but I wasn't about to throw away my one defense. I searched the patch of grass around my feet for a rock or a stick.

The sound of dry leaves crackling surprised me. Hope rose in my chest, but when I looked up, a black wolf stepped out into the open. The presence of another predator caught Mr. Kitty's attention, too.

"Just my luck," I muttered. There wasn't any sign of a pack, only the one wolf. "Lone Wolf, meet Mr. Kitty. Maybe the two of you can have dinner together."

I took my eyes off the mountain lion to try to figure out what the wolf was up to. His coat was peppered with silver around his neck, and he looked bigger than the wolves I'd seen at the zoo. His golden eyes met mine, and I could have sworn he was staring at me. I closed my eyes for a second longer than was safe, and he barked, startling me. Something inside told me to run.

Weird.

The mountain lion bounded toward the wolf. I took a chance and reached for my backpack. Before I turned away, I saw the wolf crouch down in a submissive position. The cat flew over him, creating more distance between us. Then, Lone Wolf attacked the big cat.

Unsure of who to root for, I took off.

One of the creatures yelped, but I fought the desire to look back. My feet pounded against the ground as I zigzagged through the forest. Shallow breathing caused a stitch in my side, but I pushed myself to keep the pace. My face stung from being whipped by low-hanging branches.

What had been an hour climb turned into a twenty-minute sprint down the mountain. I'd gotten off course, twisting and turning around the trees, but only by a couple dozen yards. My well-worn green station wagon waited patiently for me. I'd lovingly named the vehicle Samwise. He groaned and complained, but always came through, like the fictional character in *Lord of the Rings*.

The feeling that one, if not both, of the animals had followed me kept me panicked. I didn't waste time rummaging through my bag. I ran straight for the back door and pulled the handle. Before the door was fully open, I was inside, yanking it back closed. My hand slammed down on the lock.

Why I thought a mountain lion or wolf could open a car door was beyond me. Locking the door gave me some peace of mind.

Trying to slow my heart rate, I took several deep breaths. My backpack sat in my lap with a gaping slash across the front. I unzipped the pocket and shoved my hand into the bottom. My keys were still there. My cell phone was gone.

I couldn't call the local police department about the animal attack, and I'd lost my navigator, Siri. In reality, I knew I'd be okay. But I needed a few minutes to gather myself. I squeezed my five-ten frame between the driver and passenger seats, only to drive my left knee into the steering wheel.

"Crap!" I hollered.

My hand covered my mouth, afraid the outburst would call attention to my location. I hadn't seen any signs of the mountain lion or wolf, but I didn't want them to be able to locate me. I closed my eyes and rubbed my temples in an effort to still my mind.

I decided I didn't want to wait long enough for Mr. Kitty and Lone Wolf to find me, so I inserted my key into the ignition. Samwise grumbled in irritation.

I set my hands up on ten and two, and they were trembling. I sensed something or someone nearby, but I didn't want to look up. If the mountain lion had found me, I would run him over with my car. But the wolf had saved me. It sounded crazy.

I shook my hands in the air and squeezed my eyes shut one more time. I could find my way back to my run-down motel, and then I'd get another phone. I'd report the incident, take notes for my research, and move on to the next trail tomorrow.

A few minutes passed before I worked up the nerve to shift my car into drive, and as I pulled onto the main road, I caught a glimpse of black fur and golden eyes.

www.ingramcontent.com/pod-product-compliance
Lightning Source LLC
Chambersburg PA
CBHW051954170626
46808CB00007B/2611